Joseph Whitcomb Porter

Memoir of Col. Jonathan Eddy of Eddington, Me.

with some account of the Eddy family, and of the early settlers on

Penobscot River

Joseph Whitcomb Porter

Memoir of Col. Jonathan Eddy of Eddington, Me.
with some account of the Eddy family, and of the early settlers on Penobscot River

ISBN/EAN: 9783337377687

Printed in Europe, USA, Canada, Australia, Japan

Cover: Foto ©Andreas Hilbeck / pixelio.de

More available books at **www.hansebooks.com**

MEMOIR

OF

COL. JONATHAN EDDY,

OF

EDDINGTON, ME.:

WITH SOME ACCOUNT OF

THE EDDY FAMILY,

AND OF

THE EARLY SETTLERS ON PENOBSCOT RIVER.

_____

BY

JOSEPH W. PORTER,

BURLINGTON, ME.

AUGUSTA:

SPRAGUE, OWEN & NASH, PRINTERS.

1877.

MEMOIR.

JONATHAN EDDY, born in 1726, was the son of Eleazer and Elizabeth (Cobb) Eddy of that part of the town of Norton, now Mansfield, Mass. His father dying while he was under twenty-one years of age, Jonathan Lincoln and John Andrews were appointed Nov. 7, 1739, guardians of Jonathan and of Obadiah and Oliver, his brothers, and to "bind them out as apprentices until they come of age." June 11, 1748, the guardians' account was rendered, and the estate of their father was settled. From this time to 1755 Jonathan appears to have been in Norton. At that time he was an officer in Col. Winslow's Regiment at Nova Scotia. I have a fragment of an order book in his own hand-writing, the first date in which is June 22, 1755, and then to July 12, 1755, Camp at Fort Cumberland, N. S. I have, thus far, searched in vain in the Mass. Archives for muster rolls of his company.

In 1758, he enlisted a company of troops for the War in Canada, under the following commission :

"Province of the Massachusetts Bay.

By His Excellency the Governor :

I do hereby authorize and empower Captain Jonathan Eddy to beat his Drums any where within this Province, for inlisting volunteers for His Majesty's service, in a Regiment of Foot, to be forthwith raised and put under the command of Officers belonging to this Province for a General Invasion of Canada in conjunction with the King's *British* Troops and under the supreme command of His Majesty's Commander in Chief in *America*.

And the Colonels, with the other officers of Regiments, within this Province, are hereby commanded not to give the said Jonathan Eddy any Obstruction or Molestation herein : but on the contrary to afford him all necessary Encouragement and Assistance : for which this is a sufficient Warrant.

And the said Jonathan Eddy is hereby enjoined on Pain of my highest Displeasure, to return the names of the Men he shall inlist, and out of what particular Companies and Regiments they are inlisted, to Col. William Brattle, Adjutant General, on or before the 17th day of April next, that he may lay the same before Me.

Given under My Hand at Boston, the 27th Day of March, 1758, in the Thirty First year of His Majesty's Reign.

Th : Pownal."

In 1758 he raised a company for the Reduction of Canada, in a Regiment under the command of Thomas Doty, Esquire.

"A Muster Roll of a company of foot in his Majesty's service, under the command of Captain Jonathan Eddy, in a Regiment raised by the Province of the Massachusetts Bay for the Reduction of Canada, whereof Thomas Doty, Esquire, is Colonel." Time of service from Mar. 13th to Dec. 10, 1758 :

Jonathan Eddy, Esq., Capt., Norton.			Bartholomew Burte, Private, Norton.		
Timothy Standley, Lieut., Attleboro.			John Buck,	Private,	Gloucester.
Noah Roberson,	do	Norton.	Elijah Barney,	do	Norton.
Ebenezer Grover, Ensign.		do	Samuel Bishop,	do	Attleboro.
John King,	Sargent,	do	Thomas Burton,	do	do
James Gilbert,	do	do	Joseph Balcom,	do	do
Ebenezer Swan,	do	Attleboro.	Jeremiah Bishop,	do	do
John Penney,	do	Norton.	Solomon Briggs,	do	Norton.
John White,	Corporal.	do	Seth Cook,	do	do
Amos Sweet,	do	Attleboro.	Silas Cook,	do	do
Elisha May,	do	do	Jonathan Cattell.		
John Briggs,	do	Norton.	Stephen Carpenter,	do	Attleboro.
Amos Newland,	do	do	Hezekiah Capron,	do	do
Elisha Briggs,	Drummer.	do	Joseph Cummings,	do	do
Uriah Atherton, Private, Stoughton.			Benjamin Cole,	do	Taunton.
John Allen,	Private,	Easton.	Abial Dunham,	do	Norton.
Dariet Austin,	do	Norton.	Ichabod Dogget,	do	Attleboro.
Edward Babbit,	do	do	M. Dogget,	do	do
Nehemiah Briggs,	do	do			

A part of the Muster Roll is missing from the Massachusetts Archives—from D down.

In the early part of 1759 he raised a company in Mansfield, Mass., and vicinity, for Col. Joseph Frye's Regiment, in which he served as Captain from April 2, 1759, to Sept. 30, 1760. His Order Book from April 23d, 1759, to Dec. 31st, 1759, I have, and from it, on the cover, I take the following : "April 11th, marched from home—(Mansfield) to Landlord Robson's, Stoughton ; 12th day, to Lieut. Bents, Milton ; 13th day, to Castle William, and received our provision for 70 men, it being the * * * marched on. We went on board the 21st day of April, and drew allowance the 23d day Deto."

The Regular Order Book begins April 21st, 1759, "This day Captains Eddy, Slocomb, Angier and Cheever, embarked on Board sundry Transports for Fort Cumberland."

"April 22d. Capt. Eddy having a 3d time furnished his company Billeting Roll, went on shore to the Castle to receive the Billeting money ; (before we departed from the Castle we were sundry times mustered by the Governor and Col. Burton, attended with divers other regular officers, who not only reviewed us but also saw that every man was properly accouterred) in about two hours the Captain returned from the Castle, and brought word that the Billeting would be brought on board some time this Day."

Ap. 24. "This morning about 9 o'clock, we and the whole fleet made sail after the signal made from the Commodore, Capt. Cobb, a Sloop of 8 guns. Wind S., the people in general sea-sick, and made very Dirty Work."

Ap. 25. "Came to anchor in Casco Bay."

Ap. 28. "Pemaquid in sight. Served back allowance of Rum to the people."

Ap. 29. "Monhagin on our Starboard side."

May 1. "This day at noon, observed and found ourselves in Lattitude 43—47, one degree to the northward of Boston, the Commodore and 8 more of our Fleet astern of us, the rest of our Fleet we imagine to have put into Pemaquid."

May 2. "The people down with the Measles."

May 3. "Came to an anchor at 6 o'clock in —— Bay, almost between the point and Isle of Holt."

May 5. "At 6 this morning came too at Fort Cumberland, went ashore and lodged in Barns, the Regulars being in possession of the Barracks."

May 9. "7th Regulars left the Barracks abominable Dirty."

May 23. "Whereas the Itch increases among the soldiers of this garrison, the officers are earnestly recommended to procure Brimstone, and what else may be necessary to cure and put a stop to it."

June 17. "Last night arrived here, Sloop Sea Plower, with Government stores from Boston. Mr. Livermore the Suttler, Rev. Mr. Page, Adjutant Mr. Wetherhead, were on board."

June 22. "This evening Eleazer Everett of my company died after a long indisposition."

June 30. "Divine Service to be attended once every Sunday by all in Garrison not on Duty."

July 1. "This day entertained with a discourse by Rev. Mr. Page, from 5th chap. St. Luke's Gospel and 32d verse. This day week entertained by same Mr. Page in a Discourse from Job, 30th chap. and 23d verse."

July 3. "Rum is to be issued to the troops belonging to the province of Mass. Bay, at 10 o'clock in the forenoon."

July 7. Order from Col. Frye: "Rum will not defend the Soldiers from the inclemency of ye weather nor the attacks of Stinging insects, with which this country very plentifully abounds, as clothes would, and besides too much strong water intoxicates the Brain."

July 9. "This morning about 9 o'clock Captain Phips arrived here from Halifax, and brought news that the Fleet sailed from Lewisburgh June 12th, with Mr. Allen and sundry other passengers."

July 21. "Orders: Men shall not eat their molasses with their victuals but brew it into Beer."

July 29. "Entertained to-day by Mr. Page with a Discourse from Exodus, chap. 20 and 7th verse : Thou shall not take ye name of the Lord thy God in vain for the Lord will not hold him guiltless that taketh IIis name in Vain."

Sept. 20. Orders : "All non Commissioned Officers and private soldiers that go out shooting by vertue of the Tickets dated the 19th instant, are Daily to bring all the Game they kill in the Fort Parade, and what of it they dont want to eat themselves shall be exposed to sale in ye following manner : 1st day the Commanding Officers and Captains shall be first in purchasing ; 2d day the Subb's shall be first, and so on from day to day, changing the preference as aforesaid."

Sept. 30. "Officers and private soldiers having been accustomed to gameing at cards in the Barracks, such gameing is forbidden and to be suppressed."

Oct. 21. "Yesterday in the afternoon arrived sloops from Eastward, and brought the agreeable news of Canady's Destruction."

Oct. 22. Orders : "All Sutlers are forbidden to sell any Spirituous Liquors to any of the Garrison this Day. At 12 o'clock to-day 76 great guns were fired, as well for the King's Coronation day as the joyful news of our success at Canady, at which time every officer on the beat of the General met upon the Fort parade and Drank his Majesty's good health, &c., dureing the fireing, after which they sang God save the King ; and they, with the whole Garrison who were all assembled, save those on duty and sick, gave three cheers, at which time 20 Gallons of Rum was made in good Toddy and given to the Soldiery. At night about 6 o'clock, from the alarm posts, every man discharged his Firelock three times, except some that did not go off, and then gave three cheers, which with illuminating all the windows in the Garrison belonging to the officers, concluded the Day."

Oct. 31. "This morning Mr. Page and Mr. Livermore sailed for Boston with Capt. Innis."

Dec. 31. "Future orders Continued and Carryed into a new Book begun January 1st, 1760."

Muster Roll of Captain Jonathan Eddy's Company in Colonel Joseph Frye's Regiment from April 2, 1759, to Sept. 30, 1760, at Fort Cumberland:

Josiah King, Sergeant.
Josiah Perry, Corporal.
Ichabod Doggett, "
Alexander Foster, "
Eliphalet Briggs, Drummer.
Peter Hopkins,
David Austin,
Joshua Austin,
Elijah Burrows.
John Bates,
Geo. Brintal,
Samuel Cobb,
Samuel Day,
John Eddy,
Isaac Fisher,
Jona. Tolcott,
Z. Franklin,
John Folett,
Josiah Gilbert,
Job Gilbert,
Stephen Geary,
John Gould,
Jacob Gould,
Peter Hopkins,
William Hart,
Samuel Hunt,
Eleazer Faxon,
Abiel Knapp,

John Knapp,
Moses Knapp,
Zephaniah Lane,
Nehemiah Lincoln,
Benjamin Lewis,
Benoni Morse,
Zephaniah Morse,
Jacob Newland,
Joseph Newland,
Thomas Nason,
Nathaniel Nason,
John Robinson,
David Robinson,
A. Robinson,
Robert Randall,
Thos. Sweetland,
Penticost Stanley,
Amos Skinner,
John Salmon,
Daniel Torrey,
Benjamin Tingley,
Eliphalet Thorpe,
William Wetherell,
Elijah Wetherell.
Silas Welman, (?)
Moses Ware,
Z. Watkins.

Province of the Massachusetts Bay,

1761.   To Jonathan Eddy,   Dr.

	£	s.	d.
To 20 days' expense allowed to make up this Roll, 1-6	1	10	0
" 3 days' travel from Norton to Boston and back again at 4s	0	12	0
" 20 days' his not charged in Roll when making it up	6	8	7
	£8	10	07

Boston, Feb. 3, 1761.   Errors Excepted.

JONA EDDY.

The Lieutenants in the Company were probably Macomber, Boyden and Leonard.

Above is the Muster Roll of those who served up to the time of final discharge—30 Sept. 1760.

I find in Capt. Eddy's Order Book the names of others who were of his Company, viz: John Horn drowned April 30, 1759, on the way out. Eleazer Everett died. "John Bragg of my Co. went home Nov. 3d." "Serg. Witherell, Abiel Drake, Jonah Gay, Edward Fisher, went home Nov. 12, 1759." "Sergeant Gilbert, Edward Blanchard, Stephen Franklin, Frd. Richardson and Benjamin Hall, went home Dec. 11th, 1759. 1759, Nov. 12, says "David Robinson went home without leave," but he appears to have returned, as his name was on Muster Roll when the Company was paid off.

After his discharge in 1760, he remained at Norton until 1763, when he was in Norton, calling himself of Cumberland, N. S., in a deed,—having emigrated with his family about that time. He bought lands at Fort Cumberland, some of which are now in possession of his descendants, (1876.) He was Deputy Provost Marshal and held other offices there, remaining until the breaking out of the Revolutionary War—when he fled to the United States, leaving his family behind—and March 27, 1776, he was at Gen. Washington's Head Quarters at Cambridge. See Washington's letter to Congress, dated March 27, 1776. Extract:

"I beg leave to transmit to you the copy of a petition from the Inhabitants of Nova Scotia, brought to me by Jonathan Eddy, mentioned therein, who is now here with an Acadian; from which it appears that they are in a distressed situation, and from Mr. Eddy's account they are exceedingly apprehensive that they will be reduced to the disagreeable alternative of taking up arms and joining our enemies or of fleeing their country, unless they can be protected against their insults and oppressions. He says that their committees think many salutary and valuable consequences would be derived from five or six hundred men being sent there, as it would not only quiet the minds of the people from the anxiety and uneasiness they are now filled with, and enable them to take a part in behalf of the colonies, but be the means of preventing the Indians, of which there are a good many, from taking the side of the Government, and the ministerial troops from getting such supplies of provisions from them as they have done. How far these good purposes would be answered if such a force were sent as they ask for, it is impossible to de- .termine in the present uncertain state of things, for if the army from Boston is going to Halifax as reported by them before their departure, that or a much more considerable force would be of no avail; if not, and they possess the friendly disposition to our cause suggested in the petition and declared by Mr. Eddy, it might be of great service unless another body of troops should be sent thither by administration too powerful for them to oppose, &c., &c.

I have the Honor to be, &c."

Capt. Eddy went to Philadelphia; but Congress having more on its hands than it well knew how to attend to, declined to give him any assistance. Upon his return he called on his cousin, John Eddy, then living at Chatham, Conn. Williamson's History of Maine, vol. 2, page 451, says: "But Jonathan Eddy, a native of Norton, Mass., who had resided ten years in the vicinity of Cumberland at the head of Chigneald Bay and was Sheriff of the county, represented to the General Court that the garrison had been lessened from time to time, till the number remaining was only sufficient to take care of the artillery and military stores; and that in his opinion it might be easily taken by a small force. Though he in fact received no aid nor direct encouragement, yet he returned and projected a plan for taking the fort. To ascertain its true condition, he sent Capt. Zebulon Rowe, who visited and thoroughly examined it without exciting suspicion. Eddy next had the address by persuasive threats and promises of rewards to raise about one hundred and fifty men."

Williamson is in error in relation to the aid from Massachusetts, as Col. Eddy, by order of the General Court, Sept. 5, 1776, then sitting at Watertown, received from the Commissary General of Massachusetts supplies of ammunition and provisions.

[See Appendix A.]

Col. John Allan, a refugee from Nova Scotia, and afterwards Superintendent of the Eastern Indians, on his way from Cumberland to Machias, met Col. Eddy on board a schooner with twenty-eight men, Aug. 13, in Machias Bay, and "endeavored to induce Col. Eddy to abandon his design, but without effect." Kidder His. of Rev. War in Eastern Maine, page 12, says that Col. Eddy was impressed with the belief that he should and must be successful, and proceeded on his way and made the attack. His official report and also his letter to Col. Gorham, I give, copied from Kidder His., pp. 67, 68, 69, 70, 71, 72, 73, 74.

COL. EDDY'S LETTER OF JANUARY, 5, 1777.

To the Hon. Council & House of Representatives of the State of Massachusetts Bay :

I have endeavored to inform your Honors of some part of my Proceedings since my Departure from Boston.

I left the long wharf in Boston together with Mr. Row and Mr. How, and arrived at Newbury the second Day, where we Chartered a small Vessel to carry us to Machias, at which Place we arrived (after Many Unfortunate Accidents) in about three weeks from the time of our setting out. During my Stay at Machias I met with Col. Shaw, by whose Favor I obtained Capt. West and several other good Men, to the amount of about Twenty, to join me in the Expedition against Fort Cumberland. Then Proceeded to Passamaquoddy where I was joined by a few more ; from thence to the River St. John's, and went up the same about sixty Miles to the Inhabitants, whom I found almost universally to be hearty in the Cause,—and joined us with 1 Capt., 1 Lieut. and Twenty-five Men, as also 16 Indians ; so that our whole Force now,

amounted to Seventy two Men, and with this Party I set off
for Cumberland in Whale Boats and Canoes, and standing up
the Bay arrived in a few Days at Shepody in the sd County.
At Shepody we found and took Capt. Wallser and a Party of
thirteen Men, who had been stationed there by Col. Gorham,
Commander of the Garrison at Cumberland, for the Purpose
of getting Intelligence, &c. Thence we Proceeded to Mem-
rancook, and there had a Conference with the French, who
Readily joined us, although they saw the weakness of our
Party. We then marched 12 Miles through the woods to
Sackville, and there were met by the Committee, who Ex-
pressed their Uneasiness at seeing so few of us, and those
unprovided with Artillery. Nevertheless, hoping that Col.
Shaw would soon come to our Assistance with a Reinforcement, they unanimously joined us. The same Night I sent
off a small Detachment who marched about 12 Miles through
very bad Roads to Westcock, and there took a Schooner in
Aulack River, loaded with Apples, Cyder, English Goods,
&c., to the Amount of about £300, but finding afterwards
that she was the Property of Mr. Hall of Annapolis, who is a
good Friend to the Cause of Liberty, I discharged her. I
afterwards sent another Boat Load of Men, as a Reinforcement to the first Party, making together about 30 Men, in
Order to take a Sloop which lay on the Flats below the Fort,
loaden with Provisions and other Necessaries for the Garrison. After a Difficult March, they arrived opposite the
Sloop, on board of which was a Guard of 1 Sergt. and 12
men, who had they fir'd at our People, must have alarmed
the Garrison in such a manner as to have brought them on
their Backs. However our men rushed Resolutely towards
the Sloop up to their knees in mud, which made such a noise
as to alarm the Centry, who hailed them and immediately
called the Serg't of the Guard: The Serg't on coming up,
Ordered his Men to fire, but was immediately told by Mr.
Row that if they fired one Gun, Every Man of them should
be put to Death, which so frightened the poor Devils that
they surrendered without firing a Shot, although our People

Could not board her without the Assistance of the Conquered, who let down Ropes to our Men to get up by. By this Time the Day broke and the Rest of our party made to their Assistance in the Schooner aforementioned and some Boats. In the mean Time Came down several Parties of Soldiers from the Fort, not knowing the sloop was taken, as fast as they came were made Prisoners by our Men, and order'd on board; Among the Rest, Capt. Barron, Engineer of the Garrison, and Mr. Eagleson, who may be truly Called the Pest of Society, and by his unseasonable Drunkenness the evening before, prevented his own Escape, and occasioned his being taken in Arms. The Sloop now beginning to float and the Fog breaking away, we were discovered by the Garrison, who observing our Sails loose, thought at first it was done only with an Intent to dry them, but soon Perceiving that we were under way, fired several Cannon shot at us, and marched down a Party of 60 Men to attack us, but we were at such distance that all their Shot was of no Consequence.

We then sailed to Fort Lawrence, another Part of the Township, and there landed Part of the Stores on board the Sloop to Enable us to attack the Garrison.

Having left a small Guard on board the Sloop to secure the Prisoners, I marched the Remainder to Cumberland side of the River and Encamped within about one mile of the Fort, and was there joined by a Number of the Inhabitants, so that our whole force was now about 180 Men, but having several outposts to guard, and many Prisoners to take Care of, the Number that Remained in the Camp did not Exceed 80 men; I now thought Proper to invest the Fort, and for this Purpose sent a summons to the Commanding Officer to surrender, (a Copy of which, together with his Answer, I have Enclosed.)

Upon Col. Gorham's Refusal to surrender we attempted to storm the Fort in the Night of the 12th Nov'r with our scaling Ladders and other Accoutrements, but finding the Fort to be stronger than we imagined, (occasioned by late Repairs) we thought fit to Relinquish our Design after a heavy firing from their Great Guns and small Arms, with Intermission for

2 hours, which we Sustained without any Loss, (Except one Indian being wounded) who behaved very gallantly, and Retreated in good Order to our Camp.

Our whole Force in this Attack Consisted of about 80 Men, while the Enemy were 100 strong in the Fort, as I learned since from some deserters who came over to us; a greater number than we imagined. I must needs acquaint your Honors that Never Men behaved better than ours during the engagement—never flinching in the midst of a furious Cannonade from the Enemy.

In this Posture we Continued a Number of Days, and totally cut off their Communications with the Country, Keeping them closely block'd up within the Fort, which we Expected to take in a little Time by the Assistance of a Reinforcement from Westward. In the mean Time, on the 27th Nov'r, arrived in the Bay a Man of War, from Halifax, with a Reinforcement for the Garrison, consisting of near 400 Men, and landed on that and the day following.

Nov. 30. The Enemy to the Number of 200 Came out in the Night by a round about March, got partly within our Guards, notwithstanding we had Scouts out all Night, and about Sunrise furiously Rushed upon the Barracks where our Men were quartered, who had but just Time Enough to Escape out of the Houses and run into the Bushes where, (notwithstanding the Surprise in which we were) our Men Killed and wounded 15 of the Enemy while we lost only one man, who was Killed in the Camp.

In the midst of such a Tumult they at length proceeded about 6 Miles into the Country to the Place where they imagined our stores, &c., to be, and in the Course of their March burnt 12 Houses and 12 Barns, in some of which the greater Part of our Stores were deposited. In this Dilemma, My Party being greatly weakened by sending off many for Guards with the Prisoners, &c., and our Stores being Consumed, it was thought Proper by the Committee that we should Retreat to St. Johns River, and there make a stand till we could have some certain Intelligence from the Westward, which we hope we shall have in a short time by the Favor of the Committee, who are gone forwards. And as it appears to be the opinion of the Committee of Cumberland and St. Johns River that I should Remain here, I am determined to make a Stand at this Place till I am drove off, which I believe will not be Easily done, unless the Enemy should send a Force from Halifax by Water on Purpose to subdue this Settlement, as I am continually Reinforced by People from Cumberland and the Neighboring Counties, so that I believe we shall be able to Repulse any Party that may be sent from the Garrison at Cumberland, though I imagine we shall not be troubled by any Irruption from them this Winter, as the Reinforcement is chiefly gone, having left only about 200 Men in the Fort, and those in a bad Condition for the want of Clothing; and if 200 men could be sent us by Land this winter we could Reduce the Garrison by cutting off their Supplies of wood, which they are obliged to go 8 or 9 Miles for through a Country full of small Spruce, Fir and such like Wood, Consequently very Convenient for us to lay an Ambush, as we are perfectly acquainted and the Enemy Strangers thereto; and this your Honors may easily Conceive, as we Destroyed a Number of Houses, the Property of Friends to each Side, which lay adjacent to the Fort, and the Commanding Officer having given orders to pull them down and carry the Timber into the Fort for Firing, the Committee ordered me to Prevent it by firing them, which I did accordingly, and left them destitute of anything to burn within some Miles. On this River are a considerable Number of Indians, who are universally hearty in the Cause, 16 of whom, together with the Governor Ambrose, accompanied me in the Expedition and behaved most gallantly, but are a little uneasy that no Goods are yet arrived for them from Boston, agreeable to the late Treaty with them, which was Ratified by Coll. Shaw in Behalf of the States, and I should be very glad if your Honors would Satisfy them in this Point as soon as possible, as they have been Extremely faithful during this Contest; and if this is done I am confident I can have near 200 of them to join me in any Expedition against the Enemy. All my Transactions in this Affair have been done by the Authority of a Committee of Safety for the County of Cumberland, and many Difficulties having arisen for want of Commissions, I hope your Honors will send some blank ones for the raising of a Regiment in this Province, if the Hon. Continental Congress should think fit to Carry on the War further in this Quarter, so that Proper Regulations may be made and many disorderly actions prevented. I am, &c.,

JONATHAN EDDY.

Mangerville on the R. St. John, Jany. 5th, 1777.

[See Appendix A.]

To Joseph Gorham, Esq., Lieut. Colonel Commandt of the Royal Fencibles Americans, Commanding Fort Cumberland:

The already too plentifull Effusion of Human Blood in the Unhappy Contest between Great Britain and the Colonies, calls on every one engag'd on either side, to use their utmost efforts to prevent the Unnatural Carnage, but the Importance of the Cause on the side of America has made War necessary, and its Consequences, though in some Cases shocking, are yet unavoidable. But to Evidence that the virtues of humanity are carefully attended to, to temper the Fortitude of a Soldier, I have to summon you in the Name of the United Colonies to surrender the Fort now under your Command, to the Army sent under me by the States of America. I do promise that if you Surrender Yourselves as Prisoners of War you may depend upon being treated with the utmost Civility and kind Treatment; if you refuse, I am determined to storme the Fort, and you must abide the consequences.

Your answer is expected in four Hours after you receive this and the Flag to Return safe.

I am Sir Your most obedt Hble Servt

JONA. EDDY

Commanding Officer of the United Forces.

Nov. 10, 1776.

"Ft Cumberland 10th Novr 1776.

Sir—I acknowledge the receipt of a Letter (under coular of a Flagg of Truce) Signed by one Jona'n Eddy, Commanding officer, expressing a concern at the unhappy Contest at present Subsisting between great Britain and the Colonys, and recommending those engaged on either side to use their Endeavors to prevent the too Plentifull effusion of human Blood, and further summoning the Commanding officer to surrender this Garrison. From the Commencement of these Contest I have felt for my deluded Brother Subjects and Countrymen of America and for the many Innocent people they have wantonly Involved in the Horrors of an Unnatural Rebellion, and entertain every humane principle as well as an utter aversion to the unnecessary effusion of Christian Blood. Therefore command you in his Majesty's name to disarm yourself and party Immediately and Surrender to the King's mercy, and further desire you would communicate the Inclosed Manifests to as many of the Inhabitants you can and as speedily as possible, to prevent their being involved in the Same dangerous and Unhappy dilema.

Be assured Sir I shall never dishonour the Character of a Soldier by Surrendering my command to any Power except to that of my Sovereign from whence it orignated.

I am Sir Your most hble servt

Jos. Gorham Lt Col. Com'at

R. F. A. Commanding Officer

at Fort Cumberland."

I here give a copy of a Memorial he addressed to the General Court in 1783, which gives his views of his success:

"Commonwealth of Massachusetts—to the Honourable the Senate and House of Representatives assembled, the Petition of Jonathan Eddy Humbly sheweth that your Petitioner in the year 1776, September the 5th, did by order of the Honored Court then sitting at Watertown, Receive from the Comissary General supplies of Provision and ammunition, in

order to enable him with a Party to annoy the Enemies of
the United States, for which your Petitioner with others gave
their security to account for when called upon; and as your
Petitioner conceaves the intent and meaning of the Resolve
was that he should expend it that way, therefore after the
above supply, did proceed to the Eastward Shore and did
capture fifty six British soldiers, including two captains, one
surgeon, one church minister—besides thirteen killed, and
brot of seven that Deserted to us; all of which, excepting the
Dead, were brot into this State, and many of the Privates
enlisted into the service of the United States, the two Captains and several of the others were Exchanged for Prisoners
captured from the United States and carryed into Halifax.
Besides that morover was the means of keeping near two
thousand of the Enemy at Halifax for a considerable space,
after so that that the States had not so many to incounter
with at New York; and as your Petitioner is Confident the
Provision and ammunition was Expended for the (purpose)
it was designed for; and as your Petitioner does not Request
any thing for his own time and expences at Present, yet
Humbly requests this Honorable House would order that the
above obligations may be (cancelled) or such other ways
made void as you in your wisdom shall think best.

(1783)   JONA. EDDY."

The Government of Nova Scotia had learned his boldness
and perseverance, and endeavored to capture him by offer of
large rewards.

"At a Council holden at Halifax on the 17th Nov., 1776.
Present the Honorable the Lieut. Governor, the Hon. Charles
Morris, Richard Bulkly, Henry Morton, Jonathan Binney,
Arthur Goold, John Butler.

"On certain Intelligence having been received that Jonathan Eddy, William Howe and Samuel Rogers have been to
the utmost of their power exciting and stirring up disaffection
and rebellion among the people of the county of Cumberland, and are actually before the fort at Cumberland with a

considerable number of rebels from New England, together
with some Acadians and Indians. It was therefore resolved
to offer £200 for apprehending Jonathan Eddy and £100 for
each of the others, so that they be brought to justice. Also
£100 for apprehending of John Allan, who has been deeply
concerned in exciting the said rebellion."

"In June, 1777 an expedition was undertaken for the relief
of the people upon the River St. John and upon the borders
of the Bay of Fundy, who were friendly to the United States,
and who were reported to be harrassed or oppressed by
British emissaries. It was probably projected through the
importunity of Jonathan Eddy and his brave fugitive companions, who still believed Fort Cumberland could be easily
taken. Though the consent of Congress was obtained, the
plan, the outfit, and the expense all attached to Massachusetts. * * * * But there arose unexpected difficulties
in the prosecution of the plan, which occasioned delays and
finally an entire abandonment of the enterprise in its original
form." (Williamson His. of Maine, Vol. 2, p. 458.)

The Council of Massachusetts Bay seemed to have undi-
minished confidence in the ability of Col. Eddy, for I can
find no other person named who was to command the expedition except him. He was at Machias, Aug. 12, with a
Regimental organization, supplies, &c. He was also present
at Machias when that place was attacked by the British Fleet
Aug. 13, 14, 15, 1777, and *appears to have been in command.*
Reports concerning the Battle were made by Col. John Allan,
Col. Benjamin Foster, Maj. George Stillman, and by Col.
Eddy to the Council of the State of Massachusetts Bay. In
the reports of Allan, Foster and Stillman, no authority was
claimed by them, while that of Col. Eddy's seems to be the
Report of the Officer in command at the Battle. It is passing
strange that in all the published accounts of it, and in the
centennial celebration at Machias, May 20, 1863, no mention
was made of the name of the officer probably in command at
at that most important affair.

I give a copy of Col. Eddy's official report copied from the original in the Massachusetts Archives, and which is in some respects the most full and complete account written ;

"Machias, Aug. 17, 1777.

To the Hon. Councel of the State of Massachusetts Bay : Since my last acquainting your Honors with the Intelligence I had rec'd concerning the Enemy's Design of invading this place we have found the realities of it. Last Wednesday the 13th inst appeared in sight three ships a Brig and small Schooner coming from the Westward and standing in for the Harbor and soon after came to Anchor. One of them was a large Ship supposed to be the Rainbow of 44 guns the Milford 28 the Vulture 14 and the armed Brig Hope 6. Conceiving great Hopes of taking us by surprise the Hope stood immediately up the River attended by a Sloop and twelve boats till they came opposite to a small Battery we had about 2 miles below the falls manned with about twenty men with small arms and one 2 pounder. The Enemy attempted to land there with 6 boats and about 2 or 300 men, but failed, for our men repulsed them with some loss. Early on Thursday morning it being thick foggy weather they landed a little below the Battery on a neck of clear land in hopes of cutting off the retreat of our small Party but Col. Foster there took such Precautions in that point as rendered their hopes abortive and secured his return. The Enemy then took Possession of the Battery and burnt 2 houses and barns thereabouts, and soon after the Brig stood up the river together with the Sloop and Boats above mentioned till they came fairly in sight and within good shot of the Falls not expecting to meet with any resistance but seeing Continental Colors flying and two Breast Works fill'd with men one of them having 2 2 pounders, the other one 2 pounder and 6 swivels they began to think of retreating and accordingly got the Boats ahead to tow the Brig down. This was about sunset. I instantly detached Maj. Stillman with 30 men to attack the Boats and harass the Enemy on their retreat. The Major proceeded by Land till he got abreast of the Brig and Boats about a mile and a half below the Falls and began a heavy fire which was warmly returned for some time from the Brig with Cannon and small arms. The affair continued in this Posture till they came opposite the Battery which they had taken at first, where the Brig came to an anchor the Boats not being able any longer to keep ahead because of the incessant fire of our people which as the River is pretty narrow must do considerable Execution among the Boats. Next morning she got under way again with the Boats ahead and were again attacked by our men on both sides of the River but finally got down out of reach of small arms (but soon) ran aground so that she was left dry at Low water our people got one of the 2 pounders down and began to play upon her in this Position and hulled her several times. It is very unfortunate that we had not 1 or 2 good pieces of Cannon as by that means the Brig must have struck to us. However, having lightened her with the help of the Sloop, she got off the next high water and dropped down to the other ships, and this morning the whole came to sail and went out except the Milford. Their destination is unknown to us as yet but I shall take care to inform your honors as soon as I can procure any intelligence thereof. I must beg leave to Request an immediate supply of ammunition and provisions as what I brought with me will last but a little while having been obliged to expend a good deal in this three days siege. In all these attacks our loss is only 1 man killed and Capt. Farnsworth of my Regiment wounded but hope he will do well. Great praise is due Col. Foster and the militia under his command who gave me all the assistance I could desire and behaved extremely well, as also to Maj. Stillman and the rest of the officers and men belonging to the 2 Regiments now raising. It happened extremely well for us that Mr. Allen and Mr. Preble had arrived with about 40 Indians who were of great service to us and assisted us greatly. The Enemy's loss in all these attacks must have been pretty considerable though we cannot at present come to any certainty of it. For further particulars

I refer you to Lieut. Col. Campbell who has been very alert on this occasion and given us all the assistance in his power from the western settlements.

I am with Respect your Honors Most Obedient Humble Servant.

JONA. EDDY."

A Committee of the Town of Machias, Aug. 25, 1777, addressed Col. Eddy the following letter :

"Sir: The Inhabitants of Machias in town meeting assembled, are informed that the expedition to St. Johns in Nova Scotia is laid aside and that you have orders (to discharge) all the men belonging to your Regiment. We supposed when the Court pass'd that resolve they had no apprehension of our being attacked by our Enemies, but you are an eye witness to the late attack made upon us, and of their defeat and are also sensible that by all the information we can obtain that they are retired to collect a Superior force with a determination to destroy this place ; We the Subscribers are by the Inhabitants of Machias in their said meeting chosen as a Committee to wait upon you and request of you not to discharge any one of the enlisted men belonging to your Regiment but to consign them over to Major Stillman and to assure you that the Inhabitants of this place will be answerable for their pay and support.

We are sir with Esteem your most Obed't Humble Servants.

STEPHEN JONES,
BENJ. FOSTER,
GEO. STILLMAN,
JONAS FARNSWORTH,
STEPHEN SMITH.

To Col. Jona. Eddy, Commanding."

"The Deposition of Colonel Jonathan Eddy who testifieth and saith that on the 14th day of August 1777 he being at Machias and being commanding officer there and at the same time the place was beset by the enemy the said Deponent asked Mr. Allan Superintendent of the Eastern Indians to take his arms and head the Indians he immediately Replyed that he had not taken up arms as yet and did not Desire to and further saith not. JONATHAN EDDY."

"Suffolk, ss. July 7, 1779. Then Jonathan Eddy personally appeared and made oath to the truth of the above declaration before me.

JOSEPH GREENLEAF, Justice peace."

As there has been some controversy as to who was in command at Machias, I here insert a communication printed in the Machias (Me.) Republican, April 7, 1877, which covers the whole ground:

COL. JONATHAN EDDY.

To the Editor of the Republican:

I have your paper of Jan. 6, 1877, containing an interesting reply to my article of Nov. 25th, 1876, by George H. Allan, Esq., of Boston. I have delayed an answer in the hope that I might be able to examine some papers in the Archives of Massachusetts, which bear materially on the case, but that at present I cannot do. I honor my friend Allan for the jealous care with which he guards the reputation of his noble and patriotic ancestor, Col. John Allan, who was, up to the period we write of, Superintendent of the Eastern Indians. I have no controversy with him—I only wish to bring out the facts. One good will come out of this, and that is, that the old town of Machias will stand some chance to get its due in the history of the country.

Was Col. Jonathan Eddy in command at the battle of Machias in August, 1777? I affirm that he was, for the following reasons, and I will re-state them as briefly as I can, with such additions as I may have at hand. Col. Eddy was at Machias at the time with a Regimental organization, officers, soldiers and supplies, on his way to St. John's river and Nova Scotia with another expedition. I know not how many men he had; he was at the time recruiting men to fill up his regiment. I copy from original papers now before me :

" Boston, Sept. 18, 1777. We the subscribers do acknowledge to have Rec'd of Col. Jona. Eddy in behalf of the Paymaster of the Regiment the several sums set against our names in full, for our and our companies for services done in the Regiment under the command of the said Jonathan Eddy Esquire.   Witness our hands.

Capt. Nath. Reynolds,	£78	2	8
Zebulon Row,	49	6	7
Anthony Burk,	55	8	8
Bartholomew York,	75	19	6
Jonas Farnsworth, (not in full)	19	4	5

" Boston, Feb. 10, 1778. Rec. of Col. Jona. Eddy, Ten pounds, six shillings & sixpence ; and also rec'd of Col. Alex. Campbell, Twenty-one pounds, twelve shillings, it being in full of the wages Due me for being in the State Service in said Eddy's Regiment the summer past.

Jonas Farnsworth."

It was a respectable organization. Lieut. Col. Nevers was his officer ; Elijah Ayer was his Quarter Master. I copy from original papers :

" Machias, Aug. 14, 1777. Then rec'd of Elijah Ayer, Quarter Master of the Troops in Machias, four stands of arms for to be made use in my Militia for the Defence of the American States.   Benj. Foster."

" Return of Provisions for James Avery for his Ration from 20th July to the 18th Day of August is four weeks.
Machias, Aug. 11, 1777.   Jas. Avery.

Jas. Avery begs Col. Eddy will give order that he might draw his Provision, the 20th July was the day he arrived at Machias."

Five Captains and Companies and a pay roll of over three hundred pounds ; a large sum for those days. Mr. Allan says : "As Col. Eddy's Regiment formed a portion of the St. John's expedition and was disbanded when that enterprise was given up, Col. Allen, the commander of that expedition, must have been the first in command at the battle of Machias." I put Allan in 1777 against Allen in 1877. In

Col. Allan's letter dated Machias Sept. 22, 1777, in Kidder's most valuable history, page 229, he says : * * * "The Letter which came to Col. Eddy, (after Col. Eddy had left, J. W. P.) it being on public service, I recommended Maj. Stillman to open, when we found some Blank Commissions ; had our situation been more peaceable I would have advised them to be immediately filled up. But the appointing such officers as might be thought necessary would give umbrage to others who might so influence the men as to occasion disturbance which at present appears our business to prevent— Besides it is thought requisite to delay filling them up at present as our orders comes so immediately to *Col. Eddy who was offered the command.*"

What Command? Where? Also see Col. Allan's Letter Machias Aug. 17, 1777, (Kidder, page 211) "* * * I have apply'd to Col. Eddy to call a Court Martial to inquire in the conduct of officers and others in the expedition to St. John &c." See Col. Allan's letter Aug. 27, (Kidder, page 214) "* * * I waited upon Col. Eddy and prayed him not to be so sudden in discharging his men * * * * but he appeared inflexible and was resolved to follow the orders and instructions of the Brigadier &c." This is not the language of a commanding officer ! See Col. Allan's letter Aug. 27, 1777 (Kidder, page 213) "* * * On the 22nd inst. a boy lately belonging to the Hancock was sent on shore with a letter for exchange of prisoners. Col. Eddy (no doubt for wise reasons) thought best not to answer it." If Col. Eddy was not in command why were these proposals for an exchange of prisoners referred to him? Do these extracts show Mr. Allan to have been first in Command? Do they not show the contrary? The inhabitants of Machias had a town meeting Aug. 25, 1777, and chose a Committee of five of their first men, and instructed them to request Col. "Jonathan Eddy commanding" not to discharge his men. Col. Eddy in his official Report of Aug. 17, 1777, claims the command, and the Report sounds very much like the report of a commanding officer.

He was also recognized by the Government after the expedition to St. John was abandoned, by its sending him blank Commissions for some purpose. In no other report or letter written at that time was it claimed that any other officer had the command. In Col. Eddy's deposition July 7, 1779, he testifies that he was "commanding officer" there. As to the criticisms upon Col. Eddy relating to any former period, I have only to say that he appears to have had the continued confidence of the Government, which gave him, if not the command of the expedition, the command of a Regiment therein! Mr. Allan comes down upon me with the crushing statement that "except what appears in his own letter I do not find that Col. Eddy was really in the Battle." I submit that what I have written goes to show that Col. Eddy was in the Battle and was "commanding officer."

But to turn the tables, was Col. Allan in the Battle? If so, where is the proof? Where is the proof that he had any military command recognized there at that time, or a soldier under his orders? In what is called Col. Allan's Diary, written by Lieut. Fred Delesdernier, under date of Machias, Oct. 11, 1777, (See Kidder, page 142) is written, "yesterday Mr. Allan took command of the military, having received a colonel's commission for that purpose." And in a note at the bottom of same page Mr. Kidder adds "previous to this it is probable he had been mainly acting as Superintendent of the Indians, although he was appointed a Colonel by the Mass. government six months previous." There is no proof that at that time he was acting in any other capacity than Superintendent of the Eastern Indians. Some of those Indians took part in the Battle. In his letter of Aug. 17, 1777, (Kidder, page 204) he says " * * * I embody'd the Indians between Forty and Fifty. After I had spoken to them upon the matter they very cheerfully *went* on Service down the River." In same letter (page 206) " * * * At 10 o'clock Captain Smith with a number of white men and *all the Indians* set off &c." Col. Eddy says in his official report: "It happened extremely well for us that *Mr. Allan* and Mr. Preble had arrived with about 40 Indians who were of great service &c." Col. Eddy in his Deposition before Justice Greenleaf, July 7, 1779, says he asked *Mr. Allan, Superintendent of the Eastern Indians,* " to take his arms and head his Indians, which he refused to do." Rev. Seth Noble, minister and soldier at the Battle of Machias, afterwards first settled minister of Bangor, testified under oath, also before Justice Greenleaf at Boston July 7, 1779, that at the Battle of Machias, Aug. 14,.1777, " Mr. John Allan, Superintendent of the Eastern Indians, appeared without arms. Col. Eddy desired him to take his arms and head his Indians which he refused to do." The italics in this article are mine. In view of what I have written it seems to me that there can be but one opinion, as to *who* was the "officer commanding" at the Battle of Machias, Aug. 1777.

\ J. W. PORTER.

Burlington, March 20th, 1877.

After the attack on Machias, Col. Eddy returned to Mansfield, Mass., where he resided until 1781, when he removed to Sharon, Mass.

1781, Nov. 5. The town of Sharon "Voted not to receive as an inhabitant any of the persons hereafter mentioned who have come into the town to reside—Col. Jonathan Eddy and family from Nova Scotia and others." It was then the custom to pass such a vote to prevent the town being liable for support of persons coming in. In this case, the people of Sharon soon recovered from any fear upon that point, for May 16, 1782, "At a meeting of the Freeholders, Col. Jona. Eddy was chosen to represent them at the Great and General Court of Commonwealth of Mass. for the ensuing year."

Aug. 9, 1782. "Voted that Col. Jonathan Eddy be appointed to join the other towns in advising and making a passage for ye fish called alewives, shad and other fish passing up Neponset River."

1783, May 12. "Colonel Jonathan Eddy was chosen to represent them at the Great and General Court." He was taxed in Sharon 1781, 1782, 1783, 1784.

In 1784, he resolved to emigrate to Maine, and wrote the following letter to the inhabitants of Sharon :

"To the Inhabitants of the town of Sharon—

Gent the many singular favours bestowed on me since I had my Residence in this town—Demand my warmest acknowledgement and was I to be silent on the matter it would be a piece of ingratitude and shew that I was Destitute of humanity, but with the sincerest pleasure I return you my hearty thanks : Ever wishing that the most permanent Blessings without which no people can be happy may ever Rest on the inhabitants of the town of Sharon, but as the unnatural war which we have had have Deprived me of almost all my living, yet since the Blessings of peace has been Restored to this Country, I am now inclined to Retire to some of the uncultivated parts of the Commonwealth, where with economy, industry and frugality, with a Blessing attending my Endeavors I may still hope for a Comfortable Support for my self and family, wherefore I must now take my leave of the town well assuring them that I shall Ever Rest their assured friend and well wisher. Subscribing myself at the same time Gent your most obedient

and very humble servant

May 12, 1784.   Jona Eddy."

In August of 1784, Col. Eddy with his family removed to Township No. Ten, east side of Penobscot river, at the head of the tide. This township was afterwards known as Eddytown Plantation and incorporated into the town of Eddington 1811—named in compliment to Col. Eddy.

[See Appendix A.]

Williamson's History of Maine, vol. 2, page 515, says "Jonathan Eddy and his companions had during the war manifested so ardent and laudable an attachment to the American cause that Congress (1785) moved by their merits and sufferings particularly recommended their condition to the attention and humanity of Massachusetts. Hence the government granted to twenty of them several lots of land of different sizes, making an aggregate of nine thousand acres to be located in one body.

In 1758 Governor Pownal came to Penobscot river to locate Forts, &c. He came up the river to a point supposed to be near the mouth of the Kenduskeag, and as he relates in his diary:

"Landed on the East Side the River with 136 men and proceeded to the head of the first Falls about four and a quarter from the first Ledge. Clear Land on the left for near four miles. * * * At the Head of the Falls—Buried a Leaden Plate with the following inscription: "May 23, 1758. Province of Massachusetts Bay—Dominions of Great Britain,—Possession confirmed by T. Pownal, Govr. Erected a Flag Staff,—Hoisted the King's Colors and Saluted them." (See Me. His. Soc. Coll. VI, page 335.)

In consequence of this act of Gov. Pownal, the territory between Penobscot and St. Croix was saved to the United States by the Treaty of 1783.

The precise spot where Gov. Pownal buried his plate and took possession, was without doubt upon the land of Col. Eddy which he received under this grant, and where he afterwards lived and died.

In 1785 he bought the first vessel ever owned on "Penobscot River," the Schooner Blackbird. Her Register signed by John Avery, Jr., Secretary, and Countersigned by John cock, Governor of Mass., says she was built at Beverly, 1780, and sold by Peter Coffin, Jr., of Gloucester, May 16, 1785, to Messrs. Stephen & Ralph Cross of Newburyport, and by them sold about first of November, 1785, to Col. Eddy. She was probably a fisherman, and made several voyages to Grand Manan after Col. Eddy owned her.

He was chairman of the committee appointed to employ the first minister settled on Penobscot River, Rev. Seth Noble, June 7, 1786.

[See Appendix C.]

He was the first Magistrate on "Penobscot River."

June 19, 1790. He was appointed by Governor John Hancock "A Special Justice of the Court of Common Pleas, a Register of Probate and Wills and a Justice of the Peace and Quorum for the County of Penobscot," and qualified for all those offices by Col. Paul Dudley Sargent and Judge William Vinal.

1792, Feb. 25. He issued his warrant to Capt. James Budge, calling a Meeting of Inhabitants to organize the Town of Bangor.

[See Appendix D.]

1796, Aug. Took Acknowledgement of Treaty between Mass. Commissioners and the seven chiefs of the Penobscot Tribe of Indians.

1800. He was appointed Postmaster at Eddyton Pl., a Post route having been established there.

[See Appendix E.]

In 1801 Congress granted land to the Refugees from New Brunswick and Nova Scotia, Col. Eddy receiving as his share 1,280 acres, receiving four warrants therefor, signed by Thomas Jefferson, President, James Madison, Sec. of State, dated May 7, 1802. These lands were in the Chillicotha District, Ohio.

[See Appendix R and F.]

His business as Justice was large. The number of marriages solemnized by him were numerous.

[See Appendix G.]

Col. Eddy after a long, useful and eventful life, died in August, 1804, aged 78 years.

EDDY GENEALOGY.

William Eddye, Vicar.*

Rev. William Eddy, A. M., was Vicar of Cranbrook County of Kent in England, of Saint Dunston's church, from 1589 to 1616. He was a gentleman of much method and order in all his movements in the Parish. He was a strict Episcopalian and did very much for his church and parishioners. All the loose registers of the parish dating back from 1588, were collected, arranged and properly entered by him in a new parchment book purchased by him for the express purpose. For this service he was paid by the Parish the sum of £4. He beautifully engrossed about eighty of its folio pages besides illuminating others. The records are now (1859) in a good state of preservation. On one page therein is the following entry : "Paid that was spent in charges riding to Canterbury for to carry in the first money gathered here for Virginia."

He married Mary Foster, Nov. 20th, 1587, and among other children had

    Samuel, born 1608, who came to Plymouth, Mass., 1630.

Samuel¹ Eddy, son of Rev. William Eddy, died at Swanzey, 1688 ; m. Elizabeth ———, who died ——— 1681–82.

He came to Plymouth in ship Handmaid October, 1630, where he bought a house and land of Experience Mitchell May 9, 1631. He was taxed in Plymouth from 1632 to 1688. The latter part of his life he resided with his sons in Middle-

---

* The autograph of William Eddye, Vicar, was copied from the old Parish Registers at St. Dunston's, July 30, 1859, by R. H. Eddy, Esq., No. 76 State Street, Boston.

boro and Swanzey. In a deed made near the time of his death he names his residence as of Plymouth.

"In 1651, Elizabeth, wife of Samuel Eddy, arraigned for wringing and hanging out her clothes on Lord's Day, fine twenty shillings remitted." Old Colony Records.

"In 1660, Elizabeth Eddy summoned for travelling from Plymouth to Boston on Lord's Day—fined and held."

Their children were :

1 i John,⁴ born Dec. 25, 1637.
2 ii Zecheriah,⁸ 1639.
3 iii Caleb,⁸ 1643.
4 iv Obadiah,⁸ 1645.
5 v Hannah,³ June 23, 1647.

1 John⁸ Eddy, born Plymouth Dec. 25, 1637, was a carpenter and lived in Taunton. He married first, Susanna Paddock, Nov. 12, 1665 ; she died Mar. 14, 1671. He married second, Deliverance Owen of Braintree, May 1, 1672. He was a large Land owner in Taunton, and died there Nov. 27, 1695—his widow Deliverance surviving him many years, having married again —— Smith. Inventory of his Estate sworn to by widow Deliverance, Dec. 14, 1695.

Aug. 12, 1696. Estate divided, "To Deliverance Eddy, wife, and her son Jonathan and two of her daughters, Susanna and Patience, to Ebenezer, eldest son, Eleazer, second son, Joseph, Mary Reed, eldest daughter, Mercy Fisher, second daughter, and Hannah."

6 i Mary,³ born Mar. 14, 1667 ; married —— Reed.
7 ii John, Jan. 19. 1670.
8 iii Mercy. July 5. 1673 ; m. David Fisher of Taunton, Feb. 7. 1695.
9 iv Hannah. Dec. 6. 1676.
10 v Ebenezer, May 16. 1679.
11 vi Eleazer. Oct. 16. 1681.
12 vii Joseph. Jan. 4. 1683.
13 viii Jonathan. Dec. 15. 1689.
14 ix Susanna. Sept. 18, 1692.
15 x Patience, June 27, 1696.

2 Zecheriah⁸ Eddy, born 1639 ; married Alice, daughter of Robert Paddock, May 7, 1663. He was of Plymouth,

Middleboro and Swanzey, where he died Sept. 4, 1718. His children were :

16 i   Zecheriah,[3] b. April 10. 1664.
17 ii John,[3] Oct. 10, 1666.
18 iii Elizabeth,[3] August 3, 1670; m. Samuel Whipple of Providence. Feb. 26, 1691.
19 iv Samuel,[3] June 4. 1673.
20 v Ebenezer,[3] Feb. 8, 1676.
21 vi Caleb,[3] Sept. 21, 1678.
22 vii Joshua,[3] Feb. 21, 1681.
23 viii Obadiah,[3] Sept. 2. 1683.
     All of whom had families except Samuel.

3 Caleb[2] Eddy, born 1643 ; wife Elizabeth ——, lived in Swanzey, married a Deacon, and died March 23, 1713. His children were :

24 i Caleb,[3] b. May 29, 1672.
25 ii Samuel,[3] July 15, 1675.
26 iii Zecheriah,[3] died soon.

4 Obadiah[2] Eddy, born 1645, in Plymouth ; wife ——. His children were :

27 i John,[3] b. March 22, 1670.
28 ii Hazadiah,[3] April 10, 1672.

7 John[3] Eddy of John[2] of Samuel,[1] born Taunton Jan. 19, 1670 ; wife Hepsibah ——. He died at Tisbury, May 27, 1715, his widow died May 3, 1726. In his will he mentions daughters Abigail, Hannah Manter, and Beulah Coffin.

10 Ebenezer[3] Eddy, (of John[2]) born May 16, 1679, in Taunton ; married Mary Fisher, 1702.

In 1706 he sold Joseph Eddy a purchase right. April 7, 1713, he sold land in Norton. In 1720 he sold land to Eleazer Eddy, "both of Norton, and sons of John Eddy of Taunton, deceased." In 1727 he sold land to son Ichabod. In 1730, February 11, sold land in Norton to Thomas Morey. In 1756, June 30, testified at Taunton, being then in 78th year of his age. December 9, 1756, spoken of as deceased. Died at

Norton, Mass., between June 30 and December 9, 1756. His children were :

29 i   Eleazer,⁴ b. Feb. 2, 1703.
30 ii   Mary,⁴ Nov. 22, 1704.
31 iii   Ebenezer,⁴ April 16, 1707.
32 iv   Sarah,⁴ May 9, 1705; died June 14 same year.
33 v   Jeremiah,⁴ Feb. 28, 1709.
34 vi   Obadiah,⁴ March 16, 1711; deceased young.
35 vii   Samuel,⁴ August 24, 1712.
36 viii   Waitstill,⁴ April 4, 1715; m. Cornelius Tucker, Nov. 3, 1735.
37 ix   Ichabod.⁴

11   Eleazer,³ (of John² of Samuel¹) born Taunton, Oct. 16, 1681. He probably married first, Elizabeth Randall in Taunton, March 27, 1701, and second, Elizabeth Cobb of Taunton, Feb. 6, 1723, by Rev. Joseph Avery. He was of that part of Taunton afterward Norton, then Mansfield.

Dec. 20, 1727, he sold land to his son Caleb Eddy of Norton, for 66 pounds. March 26, 1739, Eleazer Eddy of Norton relinquishes rights in estate of honored father John Eddy of Taunton, to Joseph Eddy of Taunton, naming his honored mother, Deliverance Smith, in the deed. He made his will when about 59 years of age, Nov. 7, 1739, proved Jan. 15, 1740. " He gave to eldest son John, who liveth at Colchester, Conn., to second son Caleb all my carpenter's tools, 3d son Eleazer, 4th son Joshua, Obadiah, Jonathan and Oliver not 21 years of age. Jonathan to have new west end of house."

Inventory of Eleazer Eddy of Norton, Jan. 2, 1740. Whole amount of estate £417, 08d. 11d. ; among other articles, best suit clothes, £26 ; Hat, two pounds, 10s ; Wig, 30 shillings ; Silver Shoe Buckles, 28 shillings ; Dog, five shillings. In 1740 Jonathan Lincoln and John Andrews appointed Guardians of Obadiah, Jonathan and Oliver Eddy, to bind them out as apprentices until they come of age. Guardian account rendered June 11, 1748. The children were :

38 i   John.⁴
39 ii   Caleb.⁴
40 iii   Eleazer.⁴

41 iv Joshua.⁴
42 v   Obadiah.⁴
43 vi Jonathan.⁴
44 vii Oliver.⁴
45 viii Elizabeth; m. —— Penney.
46 ix Hannah; m. Robert Miller of Rehoboth, March 7, 1726.
47 x   Charity; m. —— Baker.

The early records of Taunton having been burned many years since, no dates of birth of children can be found.

12 Joseph³ Eddy of John,² born in Taunton Jan. 4, 1683. Wife Abigail ——, probably lived in Taunton. 1732, Feb. 5, Joseph Eddy of Taunton, bought land of Jonathan Eddy of Taunton; deed witnessed by Joseph Eddy Jr. and Azariah Eddy.

13 Jonathan³ of John,² born in Taunton Dec. 15, 1689; probably lived in Taunton. 1740, Feb. 18, Jonathan Eddy, cooper, of Taunton, for 250 pounds,—part of which I had when I gave a deed of my honored father's homestead, the rest well and truly received by Joseph Eddy of Taunton— mentions brother John, who had died in Outicroft (?) island.

24 Caleb³ Eddy of Caleb,² born May 29, 1672; married Bethiah Smith of Swanzey in Taunton in 1713. He lived in Swanzey.

31 Ebenezer⁴ Eddy of Ebenezer,³ born April 16, 1707; married Martha Leonard of Bridgewater, 1734. He and wife joined church in Norton, 1755. Their children were:

49 i   Mary,⁵ b. April, 1737.
50 ii Martha,⁵ Jan 16, 1739.
51 iii Ebenezer,⁵ May 3, 1743.
52 iv Ephraim,⁵ April 1, 1745.
53 v   Moses,⁵ April 4, 1747.
54 vi Deborah,⁵ May 14, 1750.

53 Samuel⁴ Eddy of Ebenezer,³ born August 24, 1712, died before 1761; married Sarah Page of Rehoboth April 10,

1733, by Rev. Mr. Avery of Norton. He lived in Norton. His children were :

55 i Sarah,⁵ b. 29 Dec., 1735.
56 ii Hannah,⁵ 4 June, 1739.
57 iii Charity,⁶ 4 June, 1739.
58 iv Samuel,⁵ 31 Jan.. 1741.
59 v Simeon,⁵ 30 Dec., 1742.
60 vi Freelove.⁵ 10 Sept., 1744.
61 vii Anna,⁵ 25 May, 1746.
62 viii Comfort,⁵ 25 June, 1748.

37 Ichabod⁴ Eddy of Ebenezer,³ born ——, lived in Norton ; married Joanna Herndon Feb. 9, 1727.

Son John, b. Feb. 8, 1728.

Wife baptised and joined church in Norton, 1727.

In 1727, Ebenezer Eddy of Norton, sold land to son Ichabod.

39 Caleb⁴ Eddy, son of Eleazer,³ of Norton ; wife Judith. His father deeded him land in Norton, 1727. Bought land of brother Jonathan Eddy Nov. 5, 1763. His children were :

63 i Rachel,⁵ b. June 23, 1738 ; died 1739.
64 ii Abiel,⁵ April 5, 1740.
65 iii Caleb,⁵ Jan. 25, 1742.
66 iv Benaiah,⁵ Dec. 28, 1744.
66½ v Abiathar,⁵ June 16, 1746.
67 vi Mary,⁵ Sept. 10, 1748.
68 vii John,⁵ Jan. 25. 1751.
69 viii Elijah,⁵ August 2, 1752.

42 Obadiah⁴ Eddy of Eleazer,³ of Norton ; married Lois Hicks of Taunton, July 20, 1744. His children were :

70 i Ephraim,⁵ b. Nov. 17. 1744.
71 iii James,⁵ Jan. 12, 1746.
72 iv Obadiah,⁵ March 10, 1751.

43 Jonathan⁴ Eddy of Eleazer,³ born 1726–7 ; married Mary, daughter of Dr. William Ware, May 4, 1749, by George Leonard, Esq.

[See Appendix Q.]

June 22, 1748, bought a house of George Leonard, Esq. for £50. 1755, Feb. 18, Jona. Eddy of Norton, bought land of Robert Cook of Norton, near land of heirs of Ebenezer Eddy. 1756, Jona. Eddy of Norton, gentleman, sold land to Samuel Newcomb of Norton; wife Mary signed. 1761, Oct. 23, Jona. Eddy of Norton, sold land in Norton to Elkanah Lincoln of Norton, bounded on one side by land belonging to land of heirs of Samuel Eddy, deceased. 1762, April 7, Jona. Eddy of Norton, sold to Edmund Hodges land in old township of Taunton, undivided, originally belonging to John Macomber. 1762, June 21, Jonathan Eddy of Norton, for £266 13 shillings, sold land to Samuel Hunt and Nehemiah Lincoln, both of Norton—in Norton, bounded on one side by land of Caleb Eddy; wife Mary signed. 1762, Aug. 6, Nehemiah Lincoln and Samuel Hunt both of Norton, having jointly bought homestead farm of Captain Jonathan Eddy, divided it. 1763, Nov. 5, Jonathan Eddy of Cumberland, N. S., gentleman, sold Caleb Eddy of Norton, undivided land in old township of Taunton, originally owned by John Macomber and formerly owned by Ebenezer Eddy, late of Norton, deceased; before George Leonard, Esq., in Norton, Nov. 5, 1763. In 1765, he sold Abial Atwood of Oxford, a negro wench, for 40 pounds. [Mem. When he removed to Maine, he brought a negro man with him, "Black Jack;" whether he was a slave or not, I do not know. If so, he was probably the only slave owned on Penobscot river. Maj. Robert Treat charged Col. Eddy in account Mar. 4, 1788, to upsetting an axe for "Black Jack."] In 1767, Feb. 27, bought land in Cumberland, N. S. In 1769, Feb. 14, sold land in Cumberland as Provost Marshal. After Revolutionary war settled in Sharon, Mass. Taxed there 1781-2-3-4. April 17, 1781, Elkanah Hickson sold Jonathan Eddy of Nova Scotia, estate with dwelling house and barn, for 135 pounds, in Stoughtonham—now Sharon, Mass. Paid Nath. Billings 1020 pounds in full for work at Stoughtonham furnace. In 1780, bought of Samuel Forest, Jr., "one Bing of Coal, 1100 Bushels, for 3,000 pounds, near Meletiah Ware's in Foxborough." 1782, May 8, sold Ebenezer Richardson, farmer, land in Stoughtonham, for 437 Spanish milled dollars. 1785, May 17, Jonathan Eddy of Sharon, for 106 pounds, sold James Perrigo of Wrentham, Mass., two pieces of land in Wrentham, one of 45 acres, one of six acres. Jonathan Ware witness to deed. His children, all born in what is now Mansfield, Mass., were :

73 i Jonathan,⁵ b. Jan. 28, 1750.
74 ii William,⁶ August 16, 1752,
75 iii Ibrook,⁵ Jan. 9, 1754.
76 iv Elias,⁵ Nov. 30, 1757.

Col. Jonathan Eddy died August, 1804, æ. 78 ; Widow Mary Eddy died 1814.

44 Oliver⁴ Eddy of Eleazer,³ of Seabrook county of New London, Conn., sold land and house in Norton, "which my father, Eleazer Eddy, gave me in his will, Dec 2, 1751."

73 Jonathan⁵ Eddy Jr. of Jonathan,⁴ born in Mansfield, Jan. 28, 1750 ; married Rebecca Hicks. He was cast away in the Bay of Fundy 1808. His widow was living in Sackville, N. B., 1848.

[See Appendix I.]

74 Lieut. William⁵ Eddy of Jonathan,⁴ born in Mansfield, Aug. 16, 1752 ; married Olive Morse. He was a Lieut in the Continental Army, and was killed by a shot from a British frigate while in an open boat near Eastport, May 3, 1778. He had one son :

77 i William Jr. b. in Sackville, N. S., (now N. B.) July 1, 1775.

"Sept. 27, 1777, a flag of truce was granted to bring from Nova Scotia the family of William Eddy."

75 Ibrook⁵ Eddy of Jonathan,⁴ born in Mansfield, Mass., Jan. 9, 1754. He married Lona, daughter of Samuel Pratt, 2d, of Mansfield, Nov. 2d, 1778 ; she born May 6, 1760. He went to Nova Scotia with his father in 1764, and was one of the refugees from that Province during the Revolutionary War, for which he received a grant of land in what is now Eddington, Me. He was a Deputy Sheriff in Bristol county, Mass., and resided in Mansfield until about 1785, when he removed to Maine to what is now Eddington. First wife died about 1802. He married second, Celia Wilde. He died Jan., 1834, and his second wife died May 23, 1842. His children, all of first wife, were :

78	i	Jonathan,[5]	b. Mansfield Jan. 31, 1780; died young.
79	ii	Experience,[6]	do	June 5, 1782; died July 10, 1791.
80	iii	Ware,[6]	do	May 3, 1784.
81	iv	Nancy,[6]	Eddington. August 8, 1786; m. Daniel Collins.
2	v	Rachel,[6]	do	Feb. 22, 1788; m. Moses Collins. ·
83	vi	Eleazer,[6] *	do	Oct. 10, 1789; m. Sylvia Campbell.
84	vii	Abagail,[6]	·do	Sept. 29, 1791; m. Moses Knapp.
85	viii	Mary,[6]	do	Nov. 26, 1793; m. Jesse Comins.
86	ix	Sylvia,[6]	do	August 21, 1796; m. Beriah Clapp.
87	x	Experience,[6]	do	April 19, 1800; m. George Crane.

76 Elias Eddy[5] of Jonathan,[4] born in Mansfield, Nov. 30, 1757 ; married Mary Fales. He lived and died in Eddington, Me. Their children were :

88	i	Lovina, m. Nath. Hinckley of Buffalo. N. Y.
89	ii	Betsey. m. Rev. Elisha Bedel.
90	iii	Oliver, m. Widow Gates Hathorn of Eddington; her maiden name was Mann.
91	iv	William, went to New York about 1816.
92	v	Experience, m. Capt. Wright Stockwell of Eddington.
93	vi	Mary, m. Rev. Abraham Bedel of Camden, 1832; since of Gardiner.
94	vii	Edward, was brought up by his uncle, Ibrook Eddy; and was drowned near where the corporation mills now are at Veazie, Me., in 1817.

---

* Angelina, daughter of Eleazer, born in Eddington, Me., August 5, 1818; died in Burlington, Me., April 22, 1869; married Charles S. Richardson (son of Ezra) of Burlington, Me., in 1836. He born in Jay, Me., Feb. 14, 1813. Their children all born in Burlington.

George A., b. Oct. 1, 1837; drowned July 14, 1856.

James M., March 12, 1839; died April 11, 1839.

Charles R., Dec. 31, 1840; married, lives in Bradley, Me.

Charlotte E., July 6, 1844; died August 22, 1850.

Francetta S., June 23, 1847; died August 15, 1852.

Edwin M., April 11, 1849; died August 22, 1850.

Frank W., June 15, 1851.

Adda M., April 1, 1853; married Eben Files of Gorham, Me.

77 William⁶ Eddy, Jr., of William,⁵ born Sackville, N. S., (now N. B.) July 1, 1775; died in Corinth, Me., Jan. 22, 1852; married in Eddington, Rachel P. Knapp, November 17, 1796, by Rev. Seth Noble. She was born in Mansfield, Mass., May 22, 1779, and died in Corinth July 11, 1869, aged 90 years.

I here give an article from the Bangor Jeffersonian of Feb. 10, 1852, probably written by Hon. Noah Barker.* Their children were :

---

* DIED. In Corinth, on the 22d ult., William Eddy, Esq., aged 76 yrs., 6 mos. and 22 days.

His death was occasioned by his falling through the flooring of a scaffold over the beams of his barn to the threshing-floor, a distance of 18 feet; breaking several of his bones, and causing other injuries, from which he died in a few hours after he was found. He was alone at the time of the accident, and was not discovered until about three hours, as is supposed, after the sad and painful occurrence.

Mr. Eddy was a native of Sackville, N. B., formerly "Fort Lawrence," and in the vicinity of "Fort Cumberland," to which place his father, and grandfather, the late Col. Jonathan Eddy, removed from Norton, Mass., soon after the close of the French War. Col. Eddy had served in that War, and in 1754, assisted in erecting the fortifications on the Kennebec river, called "Fort Halifax," and "Fort Western." At the commencement of the War of the Revolution, the father and grandfather of Mr. Eddy, being among the many families then living in the Province who were connected by the ties of consanguinity or interest with the people of Massachusetts, and who hoped to see that Province a member of the American Confederacy, espoused the cause of Liberty, and were both, subsequently, officers of the army, commissioned by the authority of Massachusetts. Living as they did in the enemy's country, their service became of much importance to the American cause. Among their bold and hazardous exploits, was that of attacking a vessel of 100 tons as she lay aground, in the harbor, and making a prize of her! She was richly laden with supplies and military stores for the garrison. These they conveyed to Boston. Exasperated at these "*outrages,*" as they termed them, the Provincials became desperate, and offered a reward for the heads of the "*rebels,*" and wantonly set fire to their dwellings. Finding that there was no other alternative, the patriots were compelled to leave their families in the extreme depths of distress, and, in the severities of winter, flee through the wilderness to Machias, where "they successfully arrived, half-naked and famished, having been in the woods twenty-five days." The following spring, while Lieut. Wm. Eddy, the father of the subject of this sketch, was on his way to the Province, with the intention of bringing away his family, he was recognized by a Provincial, fired upon and mortally wounded, while sailing in an open boat near Eastport, to which place his body was stealthily conveyed by one of the patriots—the *father* of the late Hon. William Delesdernier, of Baileyville—and his remains were interred by him in his own garden at Eastport. Mr. Eddy was thus left an orphan in the third year of his age. These circumstances are related to show the foundation of those habits of industry which characterized him in after life. Becoming early inured to hardships and privations, he soon learned to depend solely upon his own exertions for obtaining the means of

95 i   Jonathan Maynard, b. Eddington, Oct. 22, 1797.
96 ii   Olive M.,   do   August 15, 1799.
97 iii   Willard,   do   May 24, 1801.
98 iv   Roxanna,   do   August 16, 1803.
99 v   Sylvester,   do   Oct. 21, 1805.
100 vi   Temperance B.,   do   Feb. 9, 1815.
101 vii   Maria L., Corinth, July 27, 1818.
102 viii   Charles K.,   do   Dec. 29, 1820.

80   Ware⁶ Eddy of Ibrook,⁵ born in Mansfield, Mass.,
May 3, 1784, died Eddington, November 20, 1852. Married
first, Nancy Clapp by Park Holland, Esq., 1809; she was
born Walpole, Mass., May 3, 1784, died March 23, 1829.
Married second, Olive Foster, by Luther Eaton, Esq., April
11, 1830; she was born in Winthrop, Me., March 3, 1800.
His children, all born in Eddington, were :

103 i   Jonathan, b. August 1, 1811.
104 ii   Lucy Clapp, August 3, 1813; m. Horace Blackman Nov. 27, 1835.
105 iii   Lona Pratt, July 15. 1815; died July 23, 1818.
106 iv   Celia Wilde, Sept. 10, 1817; m. Edwin Eddy Jan. 23, 1840.
107 v   Darius W., August 17, 1819.
108 vi   Mercy Wilde, June 28, 1821; died July 4, 1821.
109 vii   Lona Pratt, August 31, 1822; died March 17, 1824.
110 viii   Nancy Clapp, Dec. 22, 1824; m. Newell Avery Jan. 3, 1843.
111 ix   Eliza Holland, Feb. 27, 1827; m. Sewall Avery May 13, 1849.
112 x   Cyrus, Nov. 8, 1830.
113 xi   Ware, April 6, 1834.
114 xii   Marion, Sept. 4, 1838; m. Ezra Richardson Dec. 1, 1865. Died
       at Saginaw, Mich., April 10, 1867.
115 xiii   Lavinia, Sept. 2, 1842; m. Henry Foster Nov. 20, 1852.

83   Eleazer⁶ of Ibrook,⁵ born in Eddington, Oct. 10, 1790;
died March 13, 1826, aged 36. Lived in Eddington, Me.

subsistence and has ever been noted for his untiring perseverance. At the age of
thirteen, Mr. Eddy bade adieu to the Province, leaving behind him his mother, an
only brother and sister, and came to Eddington, a portion of which township had been
granted by Massachusetts to his grandfather and others, in consideration of their services in the Revolution. In the autumn of 1792, Mr. E. assisted in closing up the
survey of the " twenty-one townships " west of the Penobscot river, and lying between
the Waldo patent and the Piscataquis.
He married soon after, and settled in Eddington, where, with an increasing family,
he resided till Jan. 1818, when he removed to Corinth, where by industry and frugality
he has accumulated a valuable estate, and has ever been esteemed a worthy and respectable citizen; and dies much lamented, not only by his family, who are thus
called to mourn his sudden exit, but by all who had the pleasure of his acquaintance.

Married Sylvia, daughter of Thomas and Sabara (Knapp) Campbell, March 20, 1814. She was born Nov. 14, 1793; died April 30, 1860. Their children were:

116 i   Timothy, b. Feb. 12, 1815.
117 ii Edwin, Jan. 18, 1817.
118 iii Angelina, August, 1818.
119 iv Eleazer P., ⎫ Twins. Died Oct. 7, 1834.
120 v   Henry C., ⎭ born May 24, 1821; died August 2, 1856.
121 vi Sabara, August 20, 1823; m. Wm. E. Hanson.
122 vii Ware, August 31, 1835; m. Mary E. Doten.

Widow Sylvia Eddy married Ezra Richardson of Burlington, Maine, April 30, 1860, by whom she had:

Mary Ann. b. Feb. 1, 1832; died July 9, 1854.
Cordelia P., Nov. 28, 1833; died Dec. 19, 1833.
Lloyd Quincy, May 11, 1835; m. Mrs. Mary Taylor, June, 1866.
Ezra, Nov. 7, 1838; m. Marion P. Eddy, Dec. 1, 1865.

Esquire Richardson died June 14, 1838, and his widow April 30, 1860.

90 Oliver[6] of Elias[5] Eddy; married widow Gates Hathorn, her maiden name being Mann. He lived in Eddington and died during the war of 1812, leaving two children, Curtis Eddy and Charles Eddy.

95 Jonathan M.[7] of William,[6] born in Eddington Oct. 22, 1797; married Eliza Morrill of Cornville, Me., April 3, 1825. She was born Jan. 20, 1798; died August 5, 1876. Their children are:

123 i   Henry M., b. Corinth, Jan. 16, 1826; m. Adelia A. Gammon, Sept. 29, 1853.
124 ii Lucia Ann, Corinth, August 16, 1832; m. Dr. E. A. Thompson of Dover, Me., May 13, 1858.
125 iii John Nelson, August 26, 1837; m, Emily G. Huestis, Nov. 19, 1868. Resides in Chicago.

96 Olive[7] M. Eddy of William,[6] born in Eddington, August 15, 1799, died Dec. 24, 1857; married Samuel K. Campbell, May 10, 1820.

126 i   Emeline,[8] b. Dec. 27, 1820; died 1821.
127 ii Benjamin[9] F., August 22, 1822; m. Clara R. Bryant, Feb. 7, 1847.
128 iii Olive[6] F., Corinth, Dec. 8, 1855.
129 iv Clara[8] A., Dec. 12, 1857.
130 v Hattie[8] B., Nov. 27, 1860; died Feb. 22, 1861.
131 vi Frank[9] M., June 19. 1864.
132 vii Charles[9] K., June 19, 1866.

97 Willard[7] Eddy of William,[6] born in Eddington May 24, 1801, died in Corinth June 10, 1866; married Elizabeth Goodwin of St. Albans, April 9, 1828. Their children were :

133 i   Olive Jane, b. March 4. 1830: m. Virgil Brown Jan., 1849.
134 ii Sophronia, March 21, 1834; m. Rev. Porter M. Vinton, August, 1860.
135 iii Mary E., June 21, 1860; m. Geo. P. Hueston, April 16, 1861.

98 Roxana[7] Eddy of William,[6] born in Eddington, Aug. 16, 1803; married John Campbell of Corinth, Feb. 10, 1831. Several children died in infancy.

Martin, b. June, 1837; m. Sarah J. Daniels May, 1860.

99 Sylvester[7] of William,[6] born in Eddington, Oct. 21, 1805. First, married Almira Goodwin of St. Albans, Jan. 6, 1836; she died Dec. 11, 1869. Second, married Mrs. Mehitable Williams, Dec. 17, 1871; she born Ossipee, N. H., Sept. 13, 1828. He lives in Corinth. His children are :

136 i   Francis[8] A., b. March 3, 1838; m. George V. Blackman Sept. 1859.
137 ii Hannibal[9] II., July 5, 1840: m. Mary Burnham May 4, 1870.
138 iii Holman[8] J., Sept. 19, 1847; m. Eliza Devers April 29, 1876.
139 iv Hiram[9] E., March 21, 1850.

100 Temperance[7] of William,[6] born Feb. 9, 1815, in Eddington; married Hon. Noah Barker Dec. 29, 1839, he born in Exeter, Me., Nov. 14, 1807. Their children are :

140 i   George[8] Barker, b. in Exeter June 1, 1841; m. Mary E. Latham Sept. 2. 1868, in St. George, N. B. She born in Greenfield, Me., Feb., 1851. Resides in Presque Isle.
141 ii Charles[8] V., b. in Exeter Sept. 22. 1848; m. Lzizie E. Folsom of Exeter, Me., Dec. 1. 1872. She born in Exeter. Me., April 11, 1853, and died there July, 1875, leaving one child, Noah V. Barker. The father resides in Chicago, Ill.

142 iii William E., April 18, 1852. Resides with parents on old homestead at Corinth.
143 iv Nellie Arethusa, b. July 22, 1858.

101 Maria⁷ L. Eddy of William,⁶ born in Corinth, July 27, 1818; married Thos. J. Haines of Levant, May 22, 1853. He born in Portsmouth Nov. 25, 1816. Lives in Corinth, Me. Their children are :

William T., b. August 7, 1855.
Fred A.. Sept. 12, 1859; d. Dec. 6, 1863.
Frank E., Sept. 2, 1861.

102 Charles⁷ K. of William,⁶ born in Corinth, Dec. 29, 1820; married Albina, daughter of Col. John Dunning of Charleston, July 31. 1853. Their children are :

Walter Stanley. b. Corinth, June 17, 1855.
Arthur Dunning, Ottawa, Canada. July 27, 1861.
Charles Kirk, Saginaw, Michigan. August, 1867.
Lila, Saginaw, Michigan, 1870; resides East Saginaw, Mich.

103 Col. Jonathan⁷ Eddy of Ware,⁶ born in Eddington, August 12, 1811; died in Bangor, August 24, 1865, aged 54 years, 23 days. Married Caroline, daughter of Amos and Sally (Ballard) Bailey of Milford, March 5, 1839; Mrs Eddy born in Milford, July 9, 1819.

[See Appendix Q.]

Their children are :

i   Laura⁸ M., b. Bradley, August 12, 1840; m. Edward E. Parker of Bangor, Oct. 19, 1864, and has two children.
ii   Sarah⁸ Bailey, Bradley, August 3, 1842; d. Feb. 25, 1862.
iii   Caroline⁸ M., Bradley, Oct. 11, 1844; m. Charles L. Hamblen ot Boston, June 22, 1865. and has two children.
iv   Frederic⁸ A., Bradley, August 23, 1846.
v   John⁸ Franklin, Bangor, Feb. 23, 1848; m. Lottie Whittemore of Rome, N. Y.; has two children. Resides in Bay City, Michigan.
vi   Charles⁸ F., Bangor, March 21. 1852; m. Elizabeth Genn of Bucksport, Jan. 28. 1874, and has two children.
vii   Newell⁸ Avery, Bangor, May 20, 1856; now in Yale College.

Moved from Bradley to Bangor in spring of 1847.

107 Darius[7] of Ware,[6] born August 17, 1819; married
first, Eliza Blackman of Bradley, March 5, 1849, she died
March 5, 1854; married second, Elizabeth C. Tapley in Old-
town, Feb. 13, 1855, she born in Brooksville Sept. 7, 1833.
Children :

    i   Eliza B., b. Milford, Dec. 2, 1855.
    ii Etta M.,   do   Jan. 27, 1860.
    iii Edwin H.,   do   Nov. 8, 1863.
    iv Walter D., Bangor, Jan. 6, 1870.

Removed from Milford to Bangor in 1870.

117 Edwin[8] of Eleazer,[7] born Jan. 18, 1817; married
Celia W. Eddy of Ware, Jan. 23, 1840, she born Sept. 10,
1817. Their children were :

George C., b. Jan. 24, 1841; died Feb. 20, 1843.
143 Nancy M., August 14, 1842; m. Temple E. Dorr, Feb. 8, 1866.
Ellen A., Nov. 3, 1843; m. Augustus Clark, Jan. 28, 1867; daughter b.
    April 27, 1846, died May 24, 1846.
144 Selwyn, March 25, 1847; m. Cornelia C. Hall, Sept. 21, 1869.
145 Charles A., March 15, 1849; m. Harriet L. Lane, Dec. 26, 1871.
Lucy E., April 14, 1851, died June 23, 1870.

Children all born in Bradley, Me. Removed from Bradley,
Me., to Saginaw, Mich., December, 1863.

110 Newall Avery, born in Jefferson, Me., Oct. 12,
1817, died March 13, 1877; married Nancy Clapp Eddy[8] at
Bradley, Me., Jan. 3, 1843. Subjoined is a paragraph from
Bangor Whig.* Their children are :

---

* A telegram announcing the death of Hon. Newell Avery, of Detroit, Michigan,
in that city, Tuesday evening, March 13, after a very short illness, was received on
that evening by his relatives in this city.

Mr. Avery was formerly a resident of Bradley. He came there when a young man
from his home in Jefferson, near Augusta. While a resident of Bradley and for
several years after his removal to the West, he was a member of the firm of Eddy,
Murphy & Co., of this city. He left this State for Michigan about twenty-five years
since, and has since been one of the largest operators in lumber and land in the West.
He was a member of the firm of Avery & Murphy of Detroit, Avery, Murphy & Co.,
of Chicago, and Eddy, Avery & Co., of East Saginaw, and he was also in company
with many others from this State mostly. Mr. Avery in his business has by his
sagacity and close application been very successful.

Edward O., b. Bradley, Me., Oct. 23, 1844; m. Flora Huntington, Sept. 14, 1869.

Darius N., Bradley, Jan. 10, 1846; m. Elizabeth, daughter of Chas E. Dole, Bangor. Me., June 24, 1873.

Leonard C., Bradley, Oct. 18, 1847, died 1853.

Clara A.,   do   Jan. 12, 1850.

Nannie M.,   do   May 16. 1852.

George E., Port Huron, Mich., April 18, 1854.

John H., Bradley, Me., July 29, 1855.

Horace W., Port Huron, April 12, 1858.

Nellie J.,   do   April 27, 1860.

Infant,   do   1862, died 1862.

Arthur Ware, do   1863. died 1864.

Kitty M.,   do   1866, died 1867.

Harry E., Detroit, Mich., Dec. 3, 1867.

111 Sewell Avery, b. Jefferson, Me., Feb. 2, 1824; married Eliza H. Eddy[9] at Bradley, Me., May 3, 1849. Children are :

Waldo A., b. in Bradley. May 14, 1850; m. Nellie C. Lee, at Saginaw, Mich., Feb. 18, 1871. Children—Sewell Lee, b. Saginaw, Nov. 4, 1873; Arla S.. Saginaw, May 11, 1875.

Ara L., Bradley, March 16, 1853; m. Herbert C. Sanborn, at Saginaw, Oct. 30, 1873. Child—Herbert W., b. August 15, 1874.

Idella E., Bradley, Nov. 16, 1854.

Lulie E., Bradley, Oct. 19, 1859.

Lives in East Saginaw, Mich.

118 Angeline[7] Eddy of Eleazer,[6] born August, 1818; married Charles S. Richardson of Burlington, deceased.

143 Nancy M.[9] of Edwin,[8] born August 14, 1842; married Temple E. Dorr, Feb. 8, 1866. Children :

Earth E., b. April 17, 1873.

Cora M.. May 29, 1874.

Florence C., May 30, 1876.

He was loved and respected by all who knew him, ever ready and more than willing to extend a helping hand to all worthy persons, kind hearted, genial, upright and honorable; he leaves behind him as the most precious possession of his children—his untarnished name and bright record in every walk of life.

Except that he was for one year Mayor of Port Huron, where he lived the first twelve years or so after moving to Michigan, we think he has never held public office, the cares of his extensive business requiring all his time, but he has always taken great interest in public affairs and was one of the prominent members of the Republican party in Michigan.

144 Selwin⁹ of Edwin,⁸ born March 25, 1847 ; married Cornelius C. Hall Sept. 21, 1869. Children :

Clara F., b. Feb. 14, 1873.
Ella M., April 18, 1875

145 Charles A.⁹ of Edwin,⁸ born March 15, 1849 ; married Harriet L. Lane Dec. 26, 1871. Children :

Lottie C., b. March 4, 1873.
Flora E., Nov. 18, 1874.

APPENDIXES.

A.

A Rate Bill for the Plantation called Eddinton, on Penobscot River, for the year 1791.

RESIDENTS,	TAX. s.	d.	NON RESIDENTS,	TAX. s.	d.
James Nichols.	4	1	Phineas Nevers, deceased,	8	3
Eleazer Blackman,	2	10	Ebenezer Gardner,	8	3
Widow McMahon,	1	10	Zebulon Row,	6	3
Stephen Bussell,	3	6	William Maxwell,	6	3
Patrick McMahany,	2	8	Robert Foster,	2	8
Patience Hill,	1	4	Parker Clark,	3	7
Daniel Mann,	2	2	Atwood Fales,	3	5
Samuel Grant,	1	4	Elijah Eayres,	3	1
Stephen Grant,	2	6	Rev. Seth Noble,	2	5
Alex Grant,	1	7	Samuel Rodgers,	2	5
Jacob Oliver,	2	4	Nath. Reynolds.	2	5
Daniel Spencer, Jr.,	2	2	Thos. Faulkner,	1	11
Nath. Spencer,	3	3	John Day.	1	11
Phillip Spencer.	2	2	Anthony Burk,	1	0
Nath. Spencer, Jr..	1	8	Carpenter Bradford,	1	0
Isaac Page,	1	7	John Ackley,	1	6
William Lancaster.	0	9	Jona. Eddy, Jr.,	1	0
John Rowell,	0	6	William How,	1	0
Nath. McMahon.	0	6	John Partridge,	1	11
Ibrook Eddy,	2	6			
Elias Eddy.	2	6		£6 5	11
Col. Jona. Eddy,	18	4			
William Eddy,	3	5			

10,619 acres wild land, a 3.....................£1592 5

141 acres cleared land, a 6................. 42 6

23 Oxen, £9 per yoke.................... 103 10

4 Hogs, 18............................ 3 12

19 Cows, £3 each....................... 57 0

4

9 young cattle	13	10
20 Dwelling Houses or bouts..............	60	0
3 Barns, £30...........................	90	0
1 Horse, 6.........................	6	0
	£1968	3

Twenty-six poles in the Plantation.

Col. Jonathan Lowder made out the Tax Bills for 1791 and 1792, for which he charged the Plantation 1 pound 10 shillings.

B.

Resolve, June 29th, 1775.

Land granted to

Jonathan Eddy,	1,500	acres.
Ebenezer Gardiner,	1,000	"
Zebulon Row,	750	"
William Maxwell,	750	"
Robert Foster,	550	"
Parker Clarke,	500	"
Atwood Fales,	450	"
Elijah Ayer,	400	"
William Eddy,	350	"
Phineas Never,	1,000	"
Nathaniel Reynold,	300	"
Seth Noble,	300	"
Samuel Rogers,	300	"
Thomas Forkner,	230	"
John Day,	230	"
Anthony Burk,	150	"
Bradford Carpenter,	150	"
John Eckley,	150	"
Jonathan Eddy, Jr.,	150	"
William Howe,	150	"
	9,360	"

[Copy.]   "New York, 21 April, 1785.

Sir: The enclosed is a resolution of Congress. I wish it had been more in your favor, but it is all that can be done for you here at present. The Secretary of Congress has forwarded to the Governor of Massachusetts an official copy of said resolution, yet I thought it advisable to give you this notice; no doubt you will observe it is not attested by the Secretary, (he being gone to Philadelphia) I thought it not material, as you may no doubt, if necessary, have a copy attested by the Secretary of Massachusetts. I wish you to believe that I have not been inattentive to your affairs, notwithstanding the resolution may not fully come up to your expectations.

I am with real respect, your most obedient,
                                  S. HOLTEN."
This is endorsed, Dr. Holten's letter.

C.

'   "Penobscot River, Aug. 21st, 1790.

Gentlemen: Sundry attempts have been made for a settlement between the People and myself; but all to no effect. When I settled here, I consented to accept of 20 pounds less than what was really necessary to support my family, because the People said they were poor; still, to release them of the burden, I have been at the expense to collect great part of what has been collected. Very little thanks have I had for the trouble I have been at. I was desired to draw a Bond for the People to sign for my support, which was rejected and another drawn (unbeknown to me) which hath deprived me of one half of the sum proposed. I am willing to do in this and all cases as I would be done by; but necessity constrains me to say, I *must* have my pay. I must further tell you I shall look to no other persons for a settlement but that Committee which covenanted with me on June 7, 1786, to give me seventy pounds annual salary; what you then did is as binding as a note of hand. I am sorry to take any coercive measures; but I tell you again I must have my pay immediately. I am Gentleman with due respect

To the Committee.   Your most obedient

humble servant

Superscribed.   SETH NOBLE.

To Col. Jonathan Eddy, Maj. Robert Treat, Capt. John Crosby, Mr. Elisha Nevers; and the rest of the Committee chosen to make proposals to settle the Gospel on Penobscot River June 7, 1786."

Rev. Seth Noble, the first minister settled on Penobscot river, at what is now Bangor, was the son of Thomas and Sarah (Root) Noble of Westfield, Mass.; born April 15, 1743. He married 1st, Hannah Barker at Mangerville, N. B., Nov. 30, 1775; she died at Bangor June 16, 1790. 2d wife, Mrs. Ruhama Emery, April 11, 1793. He says in his Diary: "April 10, went with Mrs. Emery to Capt. Baker's, and April 11th, was married to the widow Ruhama Emery." She died at Montgomery, Mass., 1805. 3d wife, Mrs. Mary Riddle, June, 1807. His children were :

i   Seth. b. August 5, 1777. Lost at sea Oct. 20, 1798—21.

ii   Joseph. June 13, 1783; m. Mary Ackerson June 9, 1812; died in Brighton, N. B., 1869—æ. 86.

iii   Sarah, June 1, 1785; m. Martin Bartholomew of Montgomery, Mass., Nov. 1, 1804; died there Nov. 15, 1836—51.

iv   Benjamin, June 25, 1787; married; and died in Brighton (N. B.) April 12, 1860—73.

v   Hannah, Sept. 11, 1789; twice married; and died in Amity, Ohio. Nov. 11, 1854—65.

vi   Betsey, Nov. 23, 1793; m. James Phillips June, 1808; and died in Clear Creek, Ill., Sept. 2, 1850—56.

vii   Thomas, July 28, 1795; died July 31, 1795.

viii   Polly, Sept. 26, 1796; m. Elisha Atkins, Nov. 25, 1816; died at Pleasant Valley, Porter Co., Indiana.

Mr. Noble was not a college graduate, but was a good Latin scholar. He was supposed to have first settled over the Congregational Church in Mangerville, on St. John's river, N. B., June 15, 1774. He was a patriot and a soldier as well as a minister; and the Revolutionary war breaking out he fled from New Brunswick. He was at Machias during the attack on that place by the British fleet in August, 1777, and the Sabbath after "preached a sermon on the late event." In 1779, he was appointed to a mission to the Eastern Settlements, and wrote the General Court a letter of which the following is a copy :

"Woburn, June 7, 1779.

Honored Gentlemen : I received an order for a mission to the eastern settlements yesterday by the hands of Col. Baldwin, but find its contents so much different from what I expected, must decline the undertaking. I was informed the mission was to be on the river Penobscot only, but I was misinformed. There are such a variety of Islands, and other inhabitants contiguous to the waters, those seas are so much frequented by their cruisers, that I think it too dangerous an undertaking for a proscribed person to accept of. I suppose you are not unacquainted with the amazing scarcity of the necessaries of life in those parts ; add to this the reward offered me when laid out in provision or clothing, would not purchase more than —— dollars would in 1775. From a friend to those Liberties which God and nature hath bestowed on mankind.   SETH NOBLE.

To the whole Court."

Mr. Noble is next found preaching at Augusta, 1785, where he preached sixteen Sabbaths, receiving therefor, £26. 10s ; dissatisfaction grew up, or rather the majority preferred another minister, and he left. He is next found on Penobscot river, June 7, 1786, engaging with the Committee to preach there, his installation taking place Sept. 10th, 1786, at Conduskeag Plantation. He with other refugees had land granted in Eddington. His Diary says he removed his family to New Market, N. H., Nov., 1797 ; May 21, 1798, he hired to preach there for six months. Nov. 29, 1799, left New Market for Westfield ; he supplied vacant churches in that vicinity until he removed to the adjoining town of Montgomery, Mass., where he was installed first pastor of the Congregational Church, Nov. 4, 1801. He removed to Franklinton, Ohio, in the Spring of 1806, preaching at several places in the vicinity. He died Sept. 15, 1807, aged 64.

D.

"Hancock ss. To Capt. James Budge of Bangor, in said County, Gentleman—Greeting: Whereas, an act passed the General Court, in the State of Massachusetts, February the 25th Day, in the year of our Lord one thousand seven hundred and ninety-one, incorporated into a town a certain tract of Land known by the name of Condiskeag plantation, together with the inhabitants therein, by the name of Bangor; and called on me to issue a warrant to some suitable inhabitant of Bangor, to warn a meeting of the inhabitants at some convenient time and place, to choose such officers as towns are by law required to choose in the months of March and April, annually. Therefore, in the Name of the Commonwealth you are Required to warn the above said inhabitants to meet at some convenient time and Place for the aforesaid purposes, and this shall be your Sufficient Warrant for so Doing. Given under my hand and seal this 25th Day of February, in year 1792.

JONA. EDDY, Justice of the Peace."

"Bangor, March the 12th, 1792.

In obedience to the within warrant to me Directed, I have warned the within named Inhabitants to meet at the Dwelling house of Major Robert Treat, on Thursday, the 22d day of March. JAMES BUDGE."

This is the original, but there was some mistakes in Col. Eddy's dates.

E.

"Philadelphia, March 13, 1800.

Dear Sir: I have not nor shall I forget to pay all due attentions to your business. The House of Representatives have passed a new **Post Office Bill** in which provision is made to extend the Post road from Bucktown to Eddytown, and I shall recommend you for post master at that place, and because I think you a very honest man.

I am pleased to hear that the Hon. Caleb Strong is talked of for Governor of our State.

I am dear Sir with much esteem yours,

SILAS LEE.

P. S.—I hope Mr. Strong will be voted for generally with you, and he will be supported throughout the whole District. Jona. Eddy, Esquire, Eddytown, Maine."

.

F.

"Philadelphia, May 9, 1800.

My Dear Sir : I have the pleasure to inform you that the Commissioners have reported in your favor, and a Bill has been before us and is passed to a third reading, granting you one thousand two hundred and eighty acres of the Western Lands. The value of this land I can not now tell you, some say more, some less. But you are not to get the grants till the second Tuesday of January next, and it is probable I may see you between that and the present time.

I am with much esteem yours,

SILAS LEE.

Col. Jona. Eddy."

"City of Washington, Feb. 24, 1801.

Dear Sir : I have the pleasure of informing you that a Bill has passed and now become a Law, providing for you and others ; inclosed you have a copy thereof.

This Bill was negotiated in the Senate the past session, and that was the reason why the business was not brought to a close.

Yours with much esteem,

SILAS LEE.

Jona. Eddy, Esq., Eddytown, Maine."

G.

Marriages by Col Jona. Eddy.

The dates and names I have copied from Col. Eddy's own list; the places of residence from the Clerk's certificates. The town clerks of Bangor, for several years after its incorporation, persisted in calling it Condeeskeag Plantation.

1791, April 21, John Rowell to Molly Harthorn, both of Penobscot River.

1791, Sept. 8, John Mansel to Jenny Mahaney.

1791, August, Jacob Cook to Molly Hathorn, both of Orrington.

1792, April 30, Levi Lancaster to Rebecca Mann, both of Eddington Pl.

1793, Dec. 25, Wm. Tibbetts of Kenduskeag Pl. to Mrs. Sarah Thombs of Orrington.

1793, Dec. 27, Joseph Clark Jr. to Mrs. Jane Potter, both of Condeskeag Pl.

1793, Dec. 27, Arad Mayhew to Elizabeth Clark, both of Condeskeag Pl.

1794, Aug. 31, Robert Hichborn Jr. of Bangor to Miss Jean Thoms of Orrington.

1794, Sept. 4, Enoch Eayres to widow Lydia Lovitt, both of Cobenton Pl.

1795, July 16, Ben Spencer to Hannah Stanley, both of Eddington Pl.

1795, August 19, Robert Campbell to Betsey Knapp, both of Orrington.

1796, Jan. 26, Edward Garland to Abigail Freese, both of Cobentown Pl.

1796, Jan. 28, James Campbell of Orrington to Peggy Boyd of Bangor.

1796, Oct. 11, Wm. Spencer to Huldah Page, both of Cobentown Pl.

1796, Oct. 18, Joseph Potter to Rhoda Man.

1796, Nov. 2, Stephen Page to Anna Eayres, both of Cobentown Pl.

1797, Francis Robisko to Phebe Eayres, both of Cobentown Pl.

1798, June 11, Joseph Inman Jr. to Lettice Holmes, both of Cobentown Pl.

1798, August 2, Theodore Trafton to Margaret Dennet, both of Bangor.

1798, Oct. 27, Jonathan Snow to Mary Tebbetts, both of Kenduskeag Pl.

1798, Aug. 16, Edmund Hartford to Hannah Oliver, both of Eddington Pl.

1798, Oct. 31, Wm. Reed of Cobenton Pl. to Jenny Orcutt of Orrington.

1798, David Rowell to Nancy Grant.

1799, John Brooks of Cobenton Pl. to Hannah Buzzell of Sunkhaze.

1799, Wm. Cook of Orrington to Nancy Cogswell of Eddington Pl.

1799, July 6, Gates Harthon to Hannah Mann, both of Sunkhaze.

1799, Richard Lancaster to Thankful Clark of Bangor— Pub. Oct. 5.

1799, John Brown Jr. of Belfast to widow Sarah Nesmith of Bangor.

1800, March 20, Nath. McMahan to widow Nancy Clapp, both of Eddington Pl.

1800, Oct. 27, Moses Spencer of Plantation No. 4 to Sarah Grant of Eddington Pl.

1800, Dec. 25, Gideon Horton to Miss Temperance Kenney, both of Orrington.

1800, Dec. 26, Joseph Eddy to Elizabeth Rowe, both of Eddington Pl.

1800, John Minot of Canaan to Elizabeth Palmer of Bangor.

1800, David Burton to Elizabeth McMahan, both of Eddington Pl.

1800, Dec., Wm. Cortigan to Rebecca Eayres, both of Sunkhaze.

1801, Gideon Knap to Sarah Mann, both of Orrington.

1801, Isaac Freese Jr. of Stillwater to Rebecca Harthorn of Bangor.

1803, Dec. 11, Elisha Row to Leonah Mann.

1802, Nov. 20, Samuel Bailey Jr. to Katy Dudley, both of Sunkhaze Pl.

[Jeremiah Colbum was "Clark" of Colbumtown Plantation, but he invariably spelled it Cobentown.

The printed account of the Orono Centennial Celebration of March 3d, 1874, omits the fact that Orono was first organized as Colbornton Plantation and so continued for some years.]

II.

Joseph Junin, one of the Early Merchants on Penobscot River.

In Kidder's History of the Revolutionary War in Eastern Maine and Nova Scotia, page 230, is a letter from Col. John Allan, Superintendent of the Eastern Indians, to the Council of Mass., dated Machias, Sept. 22, 1777, which says: " * * I find there is a French merchant (Mons. Lunier) settled at the head of Penobscot with a British Commission to treat with the Indians he uses every Art and means to turn them they have had many Supplys from him and I fear they have given (him) much Intelligence from time to time." In another letter dated Machias, Sept. 25, 1777, (Kidder, page   ) Col. Allan says: " * * * Since my return from St. Johns I have had several conferences with the Penobscot Indians, one in particular, when we Exchanged several strings of wampum, when I perceived from what they said and other authentic accounts, that some of the most Diabolical proceedings have been carried on on that River. Great Embezzlements of Publick Money as well as imposing on the Indians, which with the close attention of Mons. Lunier, the British Agent on the head of the river gave to his business, I saw the Body must soon be driven off." Col. Allan says under date of Machias, Oct. 20, 1779, (Kidder, page   ): "Sir, I had the Honor of writing you the 28th inst., by Capt. De Badie who went in Company with Col. (Jonathan) Lowder of Penobscot, by the Lakes, 130 miles back with four Indians in two Birch Canoes. But very Unfortunately the whole Fell into the hands of the Enemy. About the 12th Instant on the River Penobscot some Canadians, Indians and French to the number of twenty-six under the direction of Capt. Lanier who lives on the Carrying place between Penobscot and St. Lawrence. * * * This Capt. Lanier the Hon. Board may remember that I mentioned his name several times since my Being here, he is an active, Vigilent fellow and great Influence among the Indians. I was very anxious to have him Dislodged on my first coming here which (could) have easily been done then. But he has now a number of Regular Troops and Canadians with him. I dread him most at present and by his late success no doubt he will Endeavor to harass these Settlements."

There can be no doubt but that the Capt. Lanier referred to was the same man who, as Joseph Junin, was murdered in his store in Condeskeag Plantation, Feb. 18, 1791. Jona. Eddy, Justice of the Peace, issued his warrant to Abraham Tourtellot, Constable, Feb. 19, 1791, to "summon and warn thirteen men, good and lawful men, * * * to view the body of Joseph Junin, then lying dead at the house of Jacob Dennet, &c." The Jury were: Capt. Thomas Campbell, Maj. Robert Treat, Capt. James Budge, William Plympton, Robert Hichborn, Andrew Webster, Capt. John Rider, John Smart, William Hasey, Elijah Smith, Nathaniel Harlow and Abraham Allen, and were paid six shillings each. The Jury found probable cause "that one Louis Paronneau, a nephew to the deceased, is the Person that hath committed this murder." Whereupon Jonathan Eddy and Simeon Fowler, Esquires, issued their warrant Oct. 23, for the arrest of Paronneau. He was arrested by Joshua Woodman, Deputy Sheriff. I give a copy of a letter now before me:

"His Excellency the Governor the Hon. Council of the Commonwealth of Massachusetts. May it please your Excellency and Honours, Inclosed is an Inquisition taken at Condeskeag Plantation, In the County of Hancock, on the 19th day of Feb., in the year of our LORD, one thousand seven hundred and ninety-one, on the Body of a French Gentleman, known by the name of Joseph Junin, who was found inhumanly murdered in his Bed in his store, in night of the eighteenth of February, by some Person or Persons unknown, by the Discharge of a Gun which forced two Balls through his brains as he lay sleeping on his Bed; and Having Probable Cause by the Oaths of the Jury of Inquest that one Louis Paronneau, a nephew of the Deceased, is the Person that hath perpetrated this murder, Have Issued a Warrant and apprehended the said Louis, And had him under examination, and have sent him by Mittimus to Gaol, and as the property of these two Persons might not be lost I have taken, with the assistance of six men Under Oath, (viz.) Maj. Robert Treat, Mr. Robert Hichborn, Mr. William Plympton, Capt. James Budge, Mr. Jacob Dennet and John Smart (an account) of all their Effects which could be found here at his store that the Consul of France or who ever may have a Right to said things may be acquainted therewith and as there is more effects lodged in other Places on this River which is not taken account of yet but shall be as soon as Possible. Therefore some further directions from your Excellency and Honours will be most gratefully acknowledged and am with sincerity your most obedient Humble Servant,   JONA. EDDY.

Condeskeag Plantation, 23 Feb. 1791."

Paronneau asserted that his Uncle was killed by three Indians, and John Emery, Jr., Elisha Mayhew, John Dennet, John Emery, Jacob Dennet, and others were employed to search the woods for the Indians, but none were found. In the speech of Rev. Mark Trafton, at the Bangor Centennial Celebration, 1870, see printed Report, page 91, says: "The first murder committed in this town was of an old Frenchman by the name of Junion, who was a trader from Castine and had a log house and store where the steam mill now stands, near the depot. A nephew of his came into my grandfather's (Jacob Dennet) one evening, wild and excited, saying the Indians were around, and he feared they would kill his uncle. He soon left, and the report of a gun was heard, and on going to the store the old man was found dead, but no doubt existed that the nephew was the murderer; he was sent to France for trial."

This must be an error. At this time Hancock County was a new County, probably without a Jail, so that the prisoner was sent to Pownalboro Jail. I find in Maine Historical Society's Collections, Vol. 6, pp. 49, 50, the following: "Lewis Paronneau was indicted on a charge of murder of his Uncle, on the Penobscot River, what is now Bangor. The motive assigned was to gain possession of the money of his uncle. He was tried at Pownalboro, in Lincoln County. His counsel were John Gardiner, a distinguished lawyer on the Kennebec, and Gen. William Lithgow, Jr. The defence was managed with much skill by his counsel. The French Consul, then resident at Boston, came down to attend the trial and exerted all the influence he could command in favor of his countryman. The Jury returned a verdict of acquittal, although there was strong circumstantial evidence of his guilt. The trial was in the old Court House, on the banks of the Kennebec River, in what is now Dresden."

I have a "true copy of the Inventory of his goods, Feb. 23, 1791, Attest: Robert Hichborn, Jr.," with a receipt attached, given to Jona. Eddy, Esquire, by Thomas Phillips, as Attorney of "Monsieur De'Latombe, Consul General of France." The goods. consisted of a complete stock of just such goods as an Indian trader of that day would want, with not many changes to suit nowadays: Green and red baize, wide ribbons of all colors, yellow hat bands, 27 plumes, black feathers, blue broadcloth, blankets, Indian guns with large quantities of ammunition, furs of all kinds, and rum sandwiched in between everything else.

The Jury of Inquest, the men who went into the woods to search for the Indians, officers' fees for taking care of prisoner, Jacob Dennet for his trouble, and "Owen Madden for three days' writing, 18 shillings," were all paid out of the estate of the murdered man. Feb. 19, 1791, "John Holyoke, Bryant Bradley, Solomon Hathorn, John Thoms, and John Emery certify that they have 'Decently laid out the body of Joseph Junin for Interment.'" Junin was an Indian trader and

without doubt the same man who acted as British Agent on
Penobscot River during the Revolutionary War.

I.

Eastport, Passamaquoddy, April 30, 1802.

Dear Sir: I just saw Nick Simmons from Cumberland,
he Informed me that about a fortnight since he was in company with your son Jonathan, who was then in Good Health;
this is what I anticipated in my last, and I accordingly Con-
gratulate you on the Circumstance. Excuse much haste.

I am your Obet Serv

LEWIS DELESDERNIER.

J.

COLONEL AND DR. PHINEAS NEVERS,

The first physician of Bangor, was a resident of Mangerville,
Sunbury County, now New Brunswick, on the St. John river.
He was one of a Committee chosen by the inhabitants "to
make Immediate application to the Congress or General
Assembly of the Massachusetts Bay for relief under their
present Distressed Circumstances." (See Kidder's History
of Revolutionary War in Eastern Maine and Nova Scotia,
page 63.)

Aid was granted to the Patriots on the St. John's River by
the General Court, June 26, 1776. At this time he was
called Dr. Nevers, and was at various places between Mangerville and Machias from May 21, 1777, to June 18, 1777,
when Col. John Allan, Superintendent of the Eastern Indians, in a letter of that date to the Council of Massachusetts
Bay, (Kidder, page 195,) says: " * * * The bearer,
Doct. Nevers, who is a Person who has Suffered the greatest
hardships, the most part of his Interest carried off by Mr.
Gould and himself Lyable every day to be made a Prisoner,
his Character in Private Life as well as his zeal for his Country, Being a Great Instrument in Keeping the Indians Quiet

in Furnishing them with Provisions, &c., merits the friendship of every person concerned, must therefore recommend him to your Honours favors."

At the attack of the British fleet upon Machias, August, 1777, he was present and acting as Lieut. Colonel in Col. Jonathan Eddy's Regiment. I copy a letter which I found in Massachusetts Archives :

"Boston, Sept. 18, 1777.

Hon. Gentlemen : I take this Earliest opportunity to Return you my hearty thanks for the Honor you did me in appointing me Lieut. Col. of the Battalion intended to be raised under the command of Col. Eddy, and more especially for your late appointment as Lieut. Col. over the Troops ordered to be raised for the defence of Machias. I hope I shall be able to conduct my self in such a manner as will give satisfaction to your Honours and the Publick. Being obliged by the tools of Tyranny either to acknowledge George the third of Grate Briton my Rightful Lord and Sovereign and bear arms against my brethren of the United States when they pleased, or leave my family and interest at their tender mercies, (which is cruelty) I chose the latter, and have been several months spending the little cash I brought of with me. I am now rather short of that article, and am to beg that your Honours would be pleased to lend me such small sum as may be necessary in accomplishing the business your honours have been or may be pleased to appoint me to do, and you will again much oblige

Your Honours most Humble Servant

PHINEAS NEVERS."

To the Hon. Council and the House of Representatives of the State of the Massachusetts Bay.

In Col. John Allan's letter, Machias, Oct. 12, 1777, (Kidder, page 238,) he says : " * * * Lieut. Col. Nevers has not yet arrived, nor have I received any Intelligence from him. I doubt whether he will raise his men before the time is out."

I have no further account of his military services. Sometime after this he removed his family to Penobscot river, to what is now Bangor, where he practised his profession. I have an old writ wherein John Nevers, for estate of Phineas Nevers, sued Thomas Low of Bangor, for medical services rendered in 1785. As one of the Refugees from Nova Scotia during the Revolutionary War, he was a grantee of lands in what is now Eddington. I find those lands taxed in Eddytown Plantation to estate of Phineas Nevers, deceased, from 1791 to 1795. He lived near where Coombs' wharf was. The Rev. Mr. Noble held his first meeting in 1786 in the Dr. Nevers' house. He probably died in October, 1785. Rev. Mr. Noble, in a letter to his wife at New Market, N. H., from Kennebec river, dated Feb. 6, 1786, informs her that "I hear and believe it is true, Col, Nevers died in October last." Mr. Noble in his Diary, July 25, 1787, recorded the fact, "Removed my family to the widow Nevers' House."

K.

Major Robert⁵ Treat, son of Joseph⁴ and Mary Treat of Boston, born there July 14, 1752. His first wife was Mary Partridge, to whom he was married Nov. 28, 1774; she was born in Haverhill, Mass., May 5, 1757, and died in Bangor June 10, 1800. He married second, Mary, daughter of Nath. Gale, Feb. 28, 1804. His children, all born in Bangor, were:

i Joseph, b. Dec. 18, 1775; unmarried. Died 1853.
ii John, Feb. 1, 1777. Died 1777.
iii Robert, Aug. 1. 1779. Drowned on his way to Boston in a vessel October 19, 1798.
iv John Partridge, July 21, 1783; m. Rosanna Duggins 1813. Lived and died in Enfield 1857.
v Polly, Oct. 1, 1785. Died 1792.
vi Joshua, August 6, 1787; unmarried. Died Sept. 1, 1821.
vii Betsey, June 24, 1791. Died same year.
viii Samuel, June 28, 1795. Died same year.
ix Robert Henry, May 18, 1798; unmarried. Died Enfield 1843.
x Nath. Gale, March 13, 1807.
xi Mary H., April 23, 1809.
xii Elizabeth Holyoke, January 19, 1802.

Joseph Treat[4] was son of Rev. Samuel[3] Treat of Eastham, on Cape Cod, who was son of Governor Robert[2] Treat of Connecticut, who was son of Richard Treat the original settler in Massachusetts, and afterward at Weathersfield, Conn.

Major Treat came to Bangor about 1773; lived at Treat's Falls in a house built by Jedediah Preble. Said by some to have kept first store in Bangor, but probably was the second merchant in Bangor. Built the first vessel at Bangor, just below the Penjejawock stream, which was then the court end of the town. He died May 27, 1824.

L.

The Family of Amos Bailey of Milford.

Amos Bailey, born Sept. 26th, 1785, Massachusetts; married Sally Ballard; she born Oct. 14, 1788, at Bucksport, Me. (?) Children:

Anna, b. May 17, 1810; m. Alfred O. Ingersoll, Lincoln, Me. They have the family bible; address him for further particulars.

Polly, March 31, 1812. Died young in Milford.

Amos, Jan. 31, 1814. Bay City, Mich., at present time.

Sally, Nov. 23, 1815. Died in Milford when young.

Jeremiah J., August 29, 1817. Died in Bangor. Married and family; 4 children. 2 alive.

Caroline, July 9, 1819; m. Jonathan Eddy. Seven children.

Mark Trafton, May 2, 1821. Detroit, Mich., family there.

Eleanor Bird, Oct. 28, 1823; m. George W. H. Brown of Lincoln. Family in Mich. Died.

Joanna Bass, Oct. 9, 1825. Died in Milford or Sunkhaze.

Mary H., March 31, 1828; m. Joseph Heald. 3 children, 2 now alive.

Sarah Ann, Feb. 18, 1830. Died in Port Huron, Mich.

Samuel, April 23, 1832. Died in Michigan.

Adaline, Jan. 3, 1834; m. A. L. Stebbins of Port Huron, Mich., where they now live. They have 2 children, a son and daughter.

M.

Col. Gabriel Johonnot was son of Zechary and Elizabeth (Quincy) Johonnot of Boston, where he was born in 1748. He married first, Martha, daughter of Rev. Samuel Cooper of Boston, 1766, and second, Sarah Bradstreet, 1774. He

5

had one son, Samuel Cooper, by his first wife, who graduated at Harvard College in 1783; settled in Portland, where he practised law, and died in Demarara, 1806.

Col. Johonnot was a merchant in Boston. In 1773 he was one of a committee to wait on consignees of several cargoes of Tea, shipped to Boston by the East India Company, and request of them not to land or pay duties on the Tea. He was Lieut. Colonel 14th Regiment of Massachusetts, in Continental Army, known as Col. Glover's. August 15, 1774, he was chairman of a Committee appointed by the Cadets "to proceed to Salem and return to Governor Gage the Standard he had presented them." In the Massachusetts Archives is an Order of Council during the Revolutionary war, "that Col. Johonnot is ordered to report what progress he made relating to exchange of prisoners with Lord Howe."

In 1784 he was living in the town of Penobscot, (now Castine) where he was prominent in town affairs, and was the second Representative of the town to the General Court of Massachusetts. He was a prominent Free Mason at Penobscot, having been one of the charter members of Hancock Lodge at its formation, and its first Senior Warden. (See Wheeler's History of Castine, page 225.)

He removed to Hampden before 1799, where he was Secretary of Rising Virtue Lodge of Masons in 1802, and for some years after.

In 1799 he had a controversy with Eliphalet Perkins of Orrington, and struck him. A few days after Perkins had him arrested and carried before Col. Jona. Eddy on a charge of assault, &c., when Col. Johonnot produced a document, of which I give a copy, and which stopped further proceedings:

"Hancock ss: Orrington, August 5, 1799. Personally appeared Gabriel Johonnot, Esquire, and complained of himself for a breach of the peace in having struck Eliphalet Perkins, on Thursday evening, the first day of August instant, and paid a fine of twelve shillings, or two dollars, as a satisfaction to the government of Massachusetts for said breach of the peace.   SIMEON FOWLER, Justice of the Peace."

I give a copy of a letter now before me :

"Hampden, Dec. 2d, 1796.

Sir : Yours of the 30th ultimo was delivered to me by Mr. David Read; in answer to the contents would observe, that my letter to Capt. Read was founded on the direct and full assertion of Joshua Eayres, the father, and corroborated by his son, and coloring of support from another person. Mr. Eayres asserted positively that when he settled and paid for the cattle it was done by Mr. Read's giving the fullest encouragement that the warrant would be quashed and all further proceedings therein stopped, asserting that he was the prosecutor, but should not nor would not appear to support the complaint; and that you said if they settled it and paid for the hay you would warrant nothing more would be done about the warrant. If this had been a true state of the case, I conceive it would have been extorting money in the fullest degree with agravated circumstances—as I have been misinformed nothing further need be added on that head. Eayres pressed to know if nothing could be done to save his children from punishment. I told him no, the only thing to be done was for them to come forward and give security for their appearance at S. J. Ct ; when there throw themselves on the mercy of the Court, and (as you observe) the having made satisfaction for the injury, would no doubt go in mitigation of the punishment. There requires examples of rigor, that the people in that quarter may see that the laws must be observed, and that if they will not quietly submit to them they must do it by compulsion, and with the addition of fines, imprisonment, whipping, &c., &c.

I am Sir, your Humble Servant,   G. JOHONNOT.
Timo. Langdon, Esq."

This letter is written in a fair, even hand, and directed to "Timothy Langdon, Esquire, Stillwater."

Col. Johonnot died in Hampden, Oct. 20, 1820—72. His will Oct. 5, 1820, proved March 6, 1821, was witnessed by John Abbot, John Godfrey and Sarah Crosby.

N.

Commonwealth of Massachusetts,

Penobscot, April 23, 1787.

The Deposition of Jeremiah Colburn of Penobscot River in the County of Lincoln, Gentleman, on oath testifieth and saith, that on or about the 28th Day of November, 1777, John Marsh of Penobscot, in the County aforesaid, Entered on an Island called and known here by the name of Marshe's Island and took up and settled on a Certain Lot of Land for A Farm for himself; which lot includes a mill Privelege. That on or about the Last of May, 1784, Messrs. Levy Bradley, Joseph More and Daniel Jemison, all of Penobscot in said County, Did then and there agree with the said John Marsh to Build a Saw mill upon the sᵈ Privelidge included in within the Lot which the sᵈ John had Settle as aforesaid. And the sᵈ Levy, Joseph and Daniel, Did also agree with the sᵈ Marsh to Relinquish to him one Quarter Part of one saw immiediately after finished in the mill which they so built, upon Conditions that the said Marsh should Relinquish 10 Acres of Land included within said Lot so as to include sᵈ mill Previledge and upon the former conditions being fulfilled upon the sᵈ Levy, Joseph and Daniel's Part. Then the sᵈ Marsh was to give A Deed of sᵈ 10 acres as soon as he obtained a Deed from Government.   JEREᴬᴴ COLBURN.

Lincoln, ss.—Penobscot, April 23, 1787.

Then Jeremiah Colburn Personally Appeared and made oath to the above Deposition.

Before me,   JONATHAN EDDY, Justice of the Peace.

O.

Boston, 3 Feb. 1801.

Dear Sir : I shall in the first place inform you that I am well and also my Family. As to the Petition of the Inhabitants of Eddington plantation it has been taken up and Committed and they have put it over, but I shall endeavor to have it called up again and get the Business so forwarded as to have an order of Notice if it is Possible. I wish you to wright to me as soon as you can make it convenient and inform me whether the House of Mr. (or Mrs.) Clapp is sold or like to be and whether it is probable that I can have a shelter in it next Spring, and if I can not, whether there is any other House that it is likely I can get for a short time, till I Build. If not, I must take up my Quarters at Kenduskeag. My Compliments to all Friends. A Letter directed to me at Belcher's will reach me in season.

I am Dear Sir yours,   PARK HOLLAND.

Jona. Eddy Esq.

P.

"To all persons To whom this Protest shall Come, Know ye that I, Willm Boyd of Bangor, in County of Hancock, Shipwright, on the 23d of April, 1792, Did enter into Contract with Doctor Oliver Mann and Hudson Bishop, Both of Penobscot, (Castine) in Said County, to Build for them A vessel of one Hundred tuns or thereabouts, as will appear by an Instrument By them Subscribed, Baring Date as Specified above, in which Instrument the Said Oliver Mann and Hudson Bishop engage on their part to furnish me with every Material to enable me to Carry on said vessel in three weeks from the date of the above said Instrument. But to my great Damage they have not furnished me with Sufficient Timber and other necessaries according to said Contract to Carry on said work. Wherefore I, the Said Boyd, hereby protest against the proceedings of said Mann and Bishop, and against all Costs, Delays, Detentions, or any Damage of any name or nater that I may Receive or Sustain thereby. Whereunto I have Set my hand this 25th day of June, 1792.

WILLM BOYD,
and carpenters that wrought on said vessel,
JAMES BOYD,
WILLIAM PATTEN,
ROBERT CAMPBELL."

Q.

Dr. William Ware was son of John³ and Mehetable (Chapin) Ware of Wrentham, Mass., born July. 4, 1697. First wife was Zebiah Sweeting, daughter of Lewis and Zebiah Sweeting, married Oct., 30, 1728; She died Nov. 1, 1732. Second wife, Anna Hodges, Sept. 27, 1733; she died June 35, 1755, aged 51. Third wife, Lydia ———. 1729, Feb. 19, he bought a farm of John Finney, in Norton. 1734, he was admitted to church in Norton from Wrentham. 1742, wife Anna admitted to church in Norton.

He was a "Practioner of Physic" for several years, and kept a public house from 1728 to 1740. In 1750, Nov. 24, he sold out and moved to Dighton, where he died. His grave stone says, "Dr. William Ware, died June 11, 1764, aged 67 years lacking 22 days." Second wife's grave stone says, "Anna, wife of Dr. William Ware, departed this life June 25, 1755, aged 50 years, 4 months and 21 days." 1764, his will in Bristol County Records, names wife Lydia; Children— William, George, Benjamin, Mary Eddy, Lucy Talbot, Abigail, Lydia. His children were :

Mary, b. Oct. 16, 1729; m. Capt. Jonathan Eddy.
Lucy; m. Nathaniel Talbot, Jr.
William, April 27, 1731.
John, Oct. 23, 1732; died 27 Oct., 1732.
George, August 26, 1734, "a Munday about sunrise."
Benjamin, March 20, 1736-7, "a Sabbath day evening."
Anna, July 10, 1741, "being a Friday about sunsetting;" died 25 Sept., 1741. Joseph, 1756. Lydia, 1758. Abigail, 1760.

R.

[Copy.] "A Return of the Refugees of Nova Scotia, who left that Province in the year 1776, with their former and present places of Residence in the United States or Elsewhere, June, 1785 :

Names.	Former Residence.	Now Resident.
1 Jonathan Eddy,	Massachusetts,	Mass.
2 Capt. Zebulon Rowe,	do	do
3 Colo. Phineas Nevers,	do	do
4 Mr. Ebenezer Garner, (Gardner)	do	do

Names.	Former Residence.	Now Resident.	
5 Mr. William Maxwell,	Massachusetts,	Mass.	
6 Anthony Burk,	do	do	
7 Thomas Falkner,	do	do	
8 Mr. Robert Foster,	do	do	
9 Mr. William Howe,	do	do	
10 Capt. Nath. Reynolds,	do	do	
11 Lieut. Bradford Carpenter, (or Car-	do	do	
12 Rev. Mr. Noble, penter Bradford)	do	do	
13 Jonathan Eddy, (Jr.)	do	do	
14 Jonathan Nevers,	do	do	dead.
15 William Eddy,	do	do	dead.
16 Ibrook Eddy,	do	do	
17 Elias Eddy,	do	do	
18 John Day,	do	do	
19 Edward Cole,	do	do	dead.
20 Dr. Parker Clark,	do	do	
21 Ambrose Cole,	do	do	
22 Daniel Thorrington, (Thornton)	do	do	dead.
23 Edward Falkner,	do	Nova Scotia.	dead.
24 Zebulon Rowe, Jr.,	Nova Scotia,	Mass.	
25 John Eckley,	Pennsylvania,	do	
26 Samuel Sharp,	do		dead.
27 Matthew Sharp,	do		dead.
28 Joseph Sharp,	do	Penn.	
29 Robert Sharp.	do	Nova Scotia.	
30 Josiah Throop,	New York,	New York.	
31 Jonas Earle,	do	do	
32 Jonas Earle, Jr.,	do	do	
33 Mr. Daniel Earle.	do	do	
34 Robert Earle,	dq	do	
35 Nath. Earle,	do	do	
36 Mr. Atwood Fails, (Fales)	Conn.	Mass.	
37 Obadiah Ayer,	do		dead.
38 Capt. John Starr,	do	Conn.	
39 Mr. Elijah Ayres,	do	do	
40 Elijah Ayer, Jr.,	do	Mass.	
41 Deacon Simeon Chester,	do	Conn.	
42 Samuel Connor, (Connover)	do		dead.
43 Samuel Fales,	do	Mass.	
44 Capt. Samuel Rogers,	Rhode Island,	do	
45 George Rogers,	do		dead.
46 Capt. Mr. Kellhem, (Amasa)	do		dead.
47 John Kellhem,	do		dead.
48 David Jenks,	do	Mass.	
49 Christopher Pain,	do		dead.
50 Lieut. James Avery,	Conn.	Mass.	

Names.	Former Residence.	Now Resident.
51 John Allan,	Nova Scotia.	
52 Edward Handsom, (Hampson)	do	dead.
53 John Fulton,	do	Nova Scotia.
54 John McGown,	do	Mass.
55 Nath. Crawford,	do	Nova Scotia.
56 John Sibley,	do	Conn.
57 Mr. Creeth,	do	Nova Scotia.
58 John Steward,	do	do
59 Lewis LeDernier,	do	Mass.
60 David Treferil, (Terrill)	do	do
61 Thos. Turnbull,	do	On-known.

The within are those who left the Province of Nova Scotia in 1776; the remaining part of the sixty-three persons I cannot ascertain, either their Names or places of Abode.

JONA. EDDY."

Col. Eddy was indefatigable in his efforts to obtain grants of land from Congress and Massachusetts for the refugees from Nova Scotia. He made many journeys and looked at several tracts of land before settling down at what is now Eddington, Me. I give a copy of his account, &c. :

"An account of cash layd out and other supplies for the proprietors since the year and in that year 1784.

To one petition for (the next word is obscure but I call it. J. W. P.) Grand Manan and journey to look at it,			
My time in that journey, 37 days,	£11	18	0
To one other journey to Congress, expenses of that journey in cash, 12	15	7	
My time and horse, 31 days,	9	6	0
To one petition for land at Penobscot and journey to look it out, my time,	13	10	0
To 7 journeys from Penobscot to Boston in order to get it laid out,	40	12	0
1787. Laid out by Mr. Titcomb, (Samuel*) his bill was,	20	11	0
2 chain men,	2	14	0
2 more men as waiters,	2	14	0
to snow shoes and mogasins,	3	0	0
to provisions for said men,	6	10	0
petition to Congress,		18	0
My expense at Boston and waiting at Boston on the Governor,			
* * * letters to Congress,	1	10	0
1790.	£105	1	7
Interest on the above,	37	16	6 "

* Mr. Samuel Titcomb was first Surveyor of Eddington, 1794.

ERRATA.

Page 30. For James Budge read James Bridge.
" 33. Caleb Eddy was a Deacon—*not* married, &c.
" 39. Read Charles G. Richardson, *not* Charles S.
" 42. Widow Sylvester Eddy married Ezra Richardson April 11, 1831, *not* April 30, 1860.
" 46. Read Charles G. Richardson instead of Charles S.
" 55. To "This bill was negatived," add "in the Senate."
" 57. Two lines from bottom, read Wm. Costigan to Rebecca Eayres.
" 58. Read Jeremiah Colburn was Clerk, &c.